The Slave's Dream
& Other Stories

The Slave's Dream
& Other Stories

Nabil Naoum Gorgy

Translated from the Arabic
by Denys Johnson-Davies

QUARTET BOOKS

First published in English by Quartet Books Limited
A member of the Namara Group
27/29 Goodge Street, London W1P 1FD

Copyright © 1991 by Nabil Naoum Gorgy
Translation copyright © 1991 by Denys Johnson-Davies

British Library Cataloguing in Publication Data
Gorgy, Nabil Naoum
 The slave's dream and other stories.
 I. Title
 892.736

ISBN 0 7043 2776 7

Typeset by MC Typeset Limited, Gillingham, Kent
Printed and bound by
BPCC Hazell Books
Aylesbury, Bucks, England
Member of BPCC Ltd.

Contents

Introduction	vi
1. The Well	1
2. Bird Mountain	11
3. The Journey of Ra	19
4. The Thousandth Journey	31
5. The Rivalry	39
6. Lover-Narrator	45
7. The Miracle	57
8. The Slave's Dream	63
9. The Visit	69
10. The Spouse	81
11. The Sweetness of Love	85
12. The Substitute	89
13. The Inheritance	97
14. The *Maria*	103
15. Modes of Pleasure	119
16. The Tomb	127
17. Dawania	139
18. Yusuf Murad Morcos	145
19. Zenodotus of Ephesus	153
20. Love Letters	161

Introduction

An introduction to a volume of short stories by an Egyptian writer might be expected to open with a reference to early pioneers such as Mahmoud Teymour and to contemporary writers like Yusuf Idris. However in the case of Nabil Naoum Gorgy the exercise would be pointless, for what is peculiar to him – and perhaps unique in modern Arabic literature – is that he exists outside any local tradition.

It was under the influence of European, American and Japanese fiction that Nabil Naoum Gorgy started writing. Thus, while the setting for most of his stories is Egyptian, the main characters invariably Egyptian and the language in which they are written Arabic, the mind behind them is an amalgam of different cultures, the result of wide reading and extensive travels. The central character is generally an architect or an engineer – he himself qualified at Cairo University and worked in and around New York as a soil engineer for eleven years. The Egyptian countryside, a fertile ground for many of Egypt's writers of fiction, is seldom the background to his stories. When infrequently it is, Nabil Naoum Gorgy provides little local colouring: no blindfolded buffaloes work primitive modes of irrigation. The locale – be it the desert in 'The Well', or Upper Egypt in 'Bird Mountain' or 'The Journey of Ra' – is suggested in a few deft strokes: in 'The Miracle' the distant desert monastery is 'like some ocean-going vessel braced by the hawsers of the shadows of date palms.' Even detailed descriptions of characters, or the analysis of states of mind or motive, are not part of this writer's stock in trade: characters emerge through the stories, and events are left to speak for themselves.

The unexpected, the sinister, and the violent are common ingredients. The stories remind us that human beings are constantly, if unknowingly, playing with fire. This violence is not fortuitous, is not brought into being to create surprise endings – it is central to the author's view of life. He would deny that it was a pessimistic one, merely realistic. Many of the stories deal with the conflicts that exist between individuals, particularly those who live in close proximity, as in 'The Well', or with the attempt by one person to better himself at the expense of another as in 'The Inheritance' and 'Bird Mountain', or with man's innate wish to subjugate emotionally his fellow man (or woman) as in 'Dawania', 'Lover-Narrator'

Introduction

and 'Modes of Pleasure'. In them all the writer stands back and makes little or no comment, certainly no moral judgements.

The stories show a wide range of inventiveness. From where does the material for such unusual writing – at least in terms of Arabic literature – derive? The writer has given as his main literary influence an exotic trio: the Argentinian Borges, the Tangier-based American Paul Bowles and the Japanese Nobel prizewinner Kawabata. He was giving these names for the benefit of western readers to whom, for the most part, they would be familiar. He should perhaps also have mentioned other sources of influence: the Old Testament, Egyptology, Eastern religious writings, and the occult in general; most particularly he might have mentioned the writings of such Muslim mystics as Ibn Arabi and al-Niffari. A reading of 'The Thousandth Journey' for example reveals his absorption of the flavour of the rich literature of Sufism, while short passages in 'Dawania' similarly show that the writer, a Christian Copt, is well versed in the byways of Islam.

Nabil Naoum Gorgy's writings are devoid of any political or social content, another factor that distances them from any modern Arabic literary tradition. The stories contain no reference to any of the dramatic events through which Egypt has passed in its recent history. The reader of them will gain no insight into the changes brought about by Nasser's revolution, the agricultural reforms, the population explosion or the several wars against Israel – gains normally associated with the reading of foreign literature.

The influence of the three writers he himself has mentioned is clearly seen in many of these stories. The underlying darknesses and 'cold loneliness' of Kawabata's world – as one of his translators has expressed it – and the occasionally oblique dialogue are present in much of Nabil Naoum Gorgy's writing. Borges' preoccupation with the arcane and his ability to delve into the cultures of the past and come out with intriguingly cryptic stories is often emulated in the present collection. With Paul Bowles, on the other hand, he shares that sense of lurking danger that makes much of the work of both writers so disquieting. With Paul Bowles the sinister has its particular locale; it lies for the most part in the deep south of Morocco and in the minds of primitive people not yet mentally castrated by the West. The outsider enters this world at his peril; it is a world that holds its attractions just because it is fraught with unusual dangers. With Nabil Naoum Gorgy the unexpected and the violent is ever-possible. In 'The Slave's Dream' the protagonist does not have to venture into mysterious deserts to meet his unhappy destiny – it lies at a friend's house with a view of the Pyramids, just a few minutes' drive from central Cairo. It is a story all the more horrific because, unlike the professor in one of Bowles's best known stories, who through gratuitous torture is shorn of all human

Introduction

attributes, even of hope itself, the central character in Gorgy's story retains in his extremity a hope, a dream, that is of necessity extreme and by any standards unthinkable.

The characters inhabiting these stories act neither with generosity nor kindness to one another, and no unseen Power intervenes to ensure that truth and virtue finally triumph. The best and most typical of them are as disturbingly amoral as Nature.

1

The Well

Dr Imad took his binoculars from their case and looked in the direction of the dark smudge which, at this distance, looked so small and solitary. This was now the only hope he had. His car had broken down and he had all but run out of water in that bleak and never-ending desert.

'Perhaps there are some bedouin there,' he said in exasperation to his wife who was with him on their first trip together since their marriage a mere matter of months ago.

As this was Sumayya's first trip to the Oases area, also her first experience of these rough desert tracks, her reaction to the serious plight they were in angered him. He ascribed it to her silliness, her inability to comprehend their situation.

'Perhaps it's a well or a tent,' he kept repeating as he increased his pace. They had begun to descend one of the moving sand dunes that stood between them and the extensive level ground that ended at that smudge he had seen through the binoculars.

'Why don't we wait beside the car till a lorry comes by?' said Sumayya, lifting up her feet with difficulty in the sea of sand as she followed after him on an unmapped journey.

'And die alongside it?' answered Imad impatiently. 'Haven't we already been here the whole of last night and most of this morning, and the sun is now at its zenith, without a single vehicle passing by or our seeing a soul?'

He stopped for a while, then looked through the binoculars again: now a small tree could be seen at the edge of the dark-coloured smudge.

'We've missed the main track, Sumayya.' Imad repeated what he had already said to her a number of times. He had also on many an occasion throughout the night shown her on the map by the light of a torch the route which they should have followed and the other abandoned one which, for their bad luck, they had taken.

'We don't know how far off course we are.'

Suddenly Imad fell silent, for the effort of talking, together with that expended in making his way through the sand, also his state of exhaustion and anxiety, had made him dizzy. He put his hand to his heart, then sank back, seeking the support of Sumayya's arm, to seat himself on the sand.

From a dry throat he whispered: 'My blood pressure has dropped dangerously and I'm afraid I'm dying.'

The Well

After several minutes Sumayya helped him to his feet. 'Let's try to keep going.' She encouraged him to continue towards the goal he was striving for.

The husband and wife continued on their way, with Imad turning over in his mind all the likely possibilities of the situation, though without talking to Sumayya; he was tired out with talking. *It's a well or at least there could be some bedouin there who would know the way and direct us to the main road. It's difficult to accept dying in this way. Perhaps, though, there won't be anyone there. And if there is, would it be better for us to go together or for me to go first and for Sumayya to wait for me here?*

'Better take off the gold ring and watch, Sumayya,' Imad finally uttered, as he himself removed his watch and the gold chain that bore the word 'Allah'. Sumayya could find no reason for being frightened but she followed his advice so as not to increase further his bad mood.

Now the distance between them and his hope of being saved drew nearer. Alongside the tree which had now come into sight, a small, beautifully coloured tent could be seen, around which grazed several goats. Distinctly visible, too, was a circular wall round a well. Though there was no sign of water as such, the form of that stone circle stamped upon Imad's being the imprint of what he might come to regard as the happiest moment of his life.

'It's a well,' he said triumphantly. 'Thanks

be to God.' The words issued from his mouth devoutly and Sumayya seemed to hear him mutter some prayers.

'I was sure. If only we'd tried to move off at dawn without all this debilitating waiting about!'

Now the complaining, condemnatory tone had returned. Sumayya said nothing, for she was weary of listening to him; he never stopped talking about himself, his skills and previous experiences.

For her, the joy of seeing the well and the tent was related to the strange charm of the place. Ever since the car had broken down, the possibility of their dying had not crossed her mind, for they at least still had a small jerrycan of water, and also a certain amount of food.

Apart from the journey's not having been in the least enjoyable to her from the very start, neither had the preceding months. Imad knew everything, made every decision and forced it upon her. To begin with, she had tried to express her own opinion but in the end, to avoid serious troubles, she had given in to him.

Now only a few minutes separated them from the tent. There existed no sense of the presence of a human being there. Imad stretched out his hand to finger the dagger which up till now he had used to peel oranges and cut cheese. With an unconscious movement he made sure that it was in the sheath attached to the right side of his belt. 'Just to make sure,' he said to Sumayya,

The Well

who had noticed.

'I don't see any dogs . . . Could the tent be deserted?' he asked her, with a return of fear. 'But what about these goats?' he went on. But Sumayya was no longer listening, her attention held by the grandeur of the scenery. Who, amidst this vast desert, could be dwelling in the tent? How was he living?

Imad approached cautiously, clapping his hands several times and calling out. When no answer came, he glanced towards Sumayya. She went forward and gently pulled back the *kilim* that acted as a door. The place was filled with light. She looked around her till her gaze came to rest on something she made out to be the face of a man asleep in one of the corners. Though most of his face was covered, she was able to distinguish the nobility of the features. No longer in the prime of life, he was nevertheless certainly under fifty years of age. She was conscious of Imad alongside her. He clapped his hands to waken the sleeping man. 'Gently, Imad,' she cautioned him, 'the man's asleep.'

Imad called out in a loud voice: 'We've got to wake him. Sheikh of the Bedouin!'

With difficulty, the man opened his eyes and looked towards the tent opening where the two strangers stood in the bright light.

'Peace be upon you, Sheikh of the Bedouin,' Imad greeted him from where he stood by the tent opening.

'And upon you be peace,' mumbled the man, having moved the head-cloth away from his face to reveal the handsome features that had been hidden by the darkness and the covering.

The man attempted to rise but was unable to do so.

'The man's ill, Imad,' said Sumayya, moving towards him. Imad pulled her back roughly to stop her from any such rashness.

'Wait . . . O Sheikh of the Bedouin, we've lost our way and we're almost out of water. Do you have any water? Do you know where the Farafra road is? Can you get us some petrol?'

The questions followed one upon the other with the man making no reply; he had closed his eyes again and dozed off.

'The man's ill, Imad.'

Sumayya entered the tent and knelt down beside the man. 'Peace be upon you.'

With great difficulty the man opened his eyes. 'And upon you be peace.' Again he tried in vain to raise himself.

'Are you ill?' She put out her hand to feel his burning forehead that had broken out in sweat with the effort.

'This is another disaster,' Imad said to himself. 'Our rescuer needs rescuing.'

'Examine him, Imad,' Sumayya ordered.

Slowly Imad approached the two of them and, kneeling down beside the man, felt his face. 'What's the trouble? What do you feel, Hagg?'*

---

*Hagg: literally 'pilgrim', the word is also used as a term of respect to an older person.

The Well

He asked the questions hastily as he glanced at the contents of the tent which amounted to no more than a small box, a number of blankets, some firewood and two plastic jerrycans. He stretched out his hand towards one of them and lifted it up to make sure it was full. Assured by its weight, he asked: 'Is there water in the well?'

'Yes,' the man answered.

'Do you know the road to Farafra?'

'Yes.'

'Where are we? Is there any army camp nearby? Do you know anyone who might come to our rescue?'

The man repeated his attempt to raise himself. 'The camp,' he finally uttered, 'is about two hours' walk from here, westwards.'

Imad's mind was now set at rest. He stood up and indicated to Sumayya that they should leave.

'The man's ill, Imad. You must do something for him.'

'The Hagg has a fever and we don't have any medicine. Let's try to get to the army camp and on our way back we can pass by him.'

'You don't know where this camp is. We're safe now, so what's the hurry? Do we have any medicine in the car that could help him?'

'Do you realize the distance the car is from here?'

Once again the man opened his eyes and they met Sumayya's. Disturbed for an instant, her eyes reflected the passing gleam of the look he gave her.

'We must save him,' Sumayya insisted.

'There's nothing wrong with him, just a slight temperature. We must hurry before the sun sets.'

'Are we going to leave him here to die?'

'He won't die. Some of his bedouin relatives will come along. There's no time to be lost.'

The man closed his eyes, moving his head away from this exchange of words; perhaps he had lost consciousness.

'Do you know where you're going?' Sumayya asked Imad in a tone full of rejection.

'Yes – the way he described it, it's two hours to the camp.'

'What camp? It's better to spend the night here and to set off in the morning.'

'No, we must reach the camp today.'

Perhaps the man gave a moan of pain or maybe it was a feverish shudder. Going out of the tent and standing by the entrance, Imad employed the compass, from which he was never parted, to determine the direction of the north and thus where the west lay. Then, having found the direction and making ready to go, he said: 'Hurry up.'

'I shan't be going,' said Sumayya in a firm voice. 'Pass by me on your way back so as to take me with you. I'm no longer capable of walking.'

'Of course you are. Are you going to stay on alone with this stranger?' Imad enquired with disgust. 'I'll wait for you outside the tent.'

'No, I'll wait until you come back.' Sumayya spoke this time in a voice that allowed him no possibility of doubting her intention. Though she had said little he knew from her tone that there was no point in trying to dissuade her.

'You're mad. This is an act of madness,' he said in a fury. Then, as one who clears himself of all responsibility because of the patient's refusal to take the medicine, he added: 'It's up to you.'

He walked away.

Sumayya spent the whole of that night awake beside the bedouin, looking after him and moistening her scarf with water so as to bring down his temperature.

Thus the days passed while she nursed him back to health. As for Imad, he did not return.

2

Bird Mountain

In the middle of the summer the architect Maurice Banoub came across an undated document relating to a burial ground that had been bought and built on by his great-grandfather and his brother. The beautiful calligraphy in which it had been written, and the contractor's ornamental seal at the bottom of the page, together with the feel of the brittle yellow paper, evoked his delight. In addition, the name of the place made a special impression on him, for the agreement stated that the burial ground was on Bird Mountain, at a place known as Angel Monastery, and that 'the extent of the crypt should be three metres by three metres and that it should be of extremely fine workmanship'.

Owing to Maurice's infatuation with the past and family history on the one hand, and on the other with the field of architecture, he decided to make a journey to the district of

Sohag from where his father's family was descended. He had long been cut off from news of them and he hoped that he might find his way to the burial ground and so perform the duty of paying a visit to his forebears, or that he might well come across some relative who was still living there.

At Sohag, Maurice hired a private car to take him to a ferry that made the journey twice a day to the other bank. Following the advice of someone knowledgeable, he found a boy who took him to the house of his father, a tailor who still employed his toes when cutting out a garment.

It was after a difficult journey by donkey that he and the father arrived at the heights of the eastern mountain, where a monk received them at the first alleyway leading to the Angel Monastery on Bird Mountain. Here flocks of cranes would put down at the time of their return from their winter migration.

Maurice went up with the monk along a twisting pathway that hung perilously over the mountain's edge. They reached a gateway in a high wall built with great constructional skill from unbaked bricks. Inside the monastery a number of cells were arranged in rows, all surrounding a large courtyard. Behind a small church were several tombs with high stone chambers and with figurines of the local angel set above the doors.

After a long period of waiting in the reception hall, they were approached by an elderly monk who introduced himself as the head of the monastery. After greeting him – for he had learnt his name from the other monk who had accompanied him – Maurice first of all went with him on a visit to the church in order to say a prayer for the souls of his forebears. The monk took him to one of the tombs whose outer covering was made of white marble and over whose vast iron gateway was a delicately wrought statue of an angel about to ascend to the heavens. Behind the gateway Maurice saw a small garden with a fountain in the centre; though it had been neglected for many years, its mosaic work was still bright and beautiful. Around the enclosure could be seen three spacious rooms, and underneath one of them was the crypt specified in the document. When Maurice expressed a desire to go into the tomb, the head of the monastery informed him that it was padlocked and that the key was with Gabriel Effendi, its owner.

'Your relative – and you don't know him?' the elderly monk teased him. After he had said a blessing for Maurice and his deceased relatives, the monk informed him that he would be able to meet Gabriel Effendi by taking himself any weekday to the Boursa Café at Sohag's railway station.

And so it was that Maurice easily found Gabriel Effendi on arriving at the Boursa Café.

'It's incredible,' said his relative. He was an elderly man with crumbling teeth and twisted features. From the ancient overcoat in which he was enveloped on that scorching day in August there emanated a repulsive smell.

At Gabriel Effendi's insistence, Maurice reluctantly agreed to spend the night at his house. That evening the two cousins sat on the great balcony that overlooked the river in the fine palace which, as Gabriel informed him, had been the property of the forebears of their respective fathers for such a long time.

'Hanna and Ishaq and Ibrahim and Samaan and Katrina and Shagara and Haniyya and Shalomet and Mathias and Bishara – all of whom have died,' said Gabriel to Maurice, examining him from behind his thick glasses that made things look like flat coloured surfaces. 'As for those at the monastery,' he continued with a cough, 'they are saints, they have put two relatives in touch with each other.'

Thus did Maurice return home from his journey to Sohag full of apprehensive thoughts, pursued by all kinds of imaginings. 'While the tomb is wonderful, the palace is a real dream.' His mind began working quickly. 'And this senile old man Gabriel, so difficult to approach because of his loathsome smell and repellent appearance, has only one foot in life and the other in the next world. After his death, seeing that he has no son or daughter or family, to whom will this palace and estate go?' Perhaps this piece of paper that had come to him so unexpectedly, showing him the way to a forgotten tomb, was really the key to an immense fortune which might have slipped through his hands had it not been for this pure coincidence.

On his return to Cairo, Maurice searched among his father's papers in the drawers in which he kept some of the photographs he had inherited. He tried to tie things together, to solve the mysteries of the family tree, but he came across no document relating to land or property apart from some ancient files containing various accounts, notebooks and medical prescriptions dating back to the time of his grandfather.

The image of the palace with its wide marble-floored balcony looking over the river, and the vast green fields that spread out on every side, continued to inhabit Maurice's imagination. There was no reason for disquiet about this fortune, for he seemed to be the sole heir, unless some third person were to make an appearance or Gabriel were to marry.

Before three days had gone by Maurice had returned to his relative Gabriel Effendi on the pretext of presenting him with some photographs relating to the family.

Maurice spent a week staying with Gabriel Effendi at the palace, going with him each morning on foot under the scorching sun to the café. It was here that trucks would deliver their loads of different makes of cigarette.

Gabriel Effendi, who was the agent in Upper Egypt for several cigarette companies, would go through numerous inventories in the names of shopkeepers in the towns and villages: the quantities, the amounts sold, expenditures, monies given as security, monies borrowed, amounts paid, and the like. And when the time for lunch came round, Gabriel Effendi would order a quick meal of beans and *falafel* sandwiches from a cart nearby the café, after which they would drink their only cup of tea for the whole day. At night, the two of them would return to the palace to be eaten by mosquitoes, for the netting that used to keep them out in olden times had come to pieces. The greater part of the evening and night Maurice would spend reading the papers and parts of the Gospels to Gabriel Effendi by the faint light of a lamp.

They did not exchange any conversation about personal matters. Gabriel Effendi did not ask him about his work, his family, or his life in Cairo, about what he felt or what his ambitions were. Likewise, Maurice tried to refrain from asking any questions or showing any surprise.

At the beginning of the second week, there was such an increase in the heat that the walk between the palace and the café seemed even longer, and Maurice felt a slight vertigo and a certain stomach upset. This he attributed to the poor diet he was having and to lack of sleep. On the final day of the same week he was unable to go with his relative to the café and took to his bed with a fever.

Gabriel Effendi was extremely distressed at his relative falling ill and he returned before midday with the district's leading doctor who gave Maurice a thorough examination. On leaving, the doctor advised him of the necessity of keeping to his bed for several weeks.

For Maurice the days passed as if they were months. Whenever he came out of the grip of the fever and recollected where he was, he would be seized with regret at having made this ill-omened visit to remote parts where the sun beat down and the flies had the upper hand over humans. Were it not for Gabriel's affection and concern, he would have died in that god-forsaken place where his unknown forebears had dwelt. 'God curse my stupidity,' Maurice secretly said to himself whenever he recollected his flat in Cairo and his evenings with his friends at the club.

At the start of the third month, as the doctor had expected, the intensity of the illness decreased and Maurice's temperature dropped. Gradually he began to get his appetite back for the food that Gabriel Effendi was cooking with the assistance of a young woman of pleasing appearance. Maurice had first became aware of her on that day when he had heard the doctor addressing her with the words, 'Our young architect still needs at least another week of rest, Madame Widad.'

When he had completely recovered and was once again sitting with Gabriel Effendi on the balcony, Madame Widad would sit with them. She was showing the first signs of pregnancy from her loving husband, who had married her because of the devotion and unselfishness she had shown from the very moment she began to nurse his cousin.

Before the passing of two months after his complete recovery, there was performed at the Angel Monastery the burial service for Madame Widad. She had passed away, together with her unborn child, after a swift illness which the doctors had been unable to diagnose. How bitterly did Gabriel Effendi weep on the shoulder of his cousin the architect Maurice Banoub, his sole heir, as they stood inside the crypt which measured three metres by three metres and was of extremely fine workmanship.

3

The Journey of Ra

The train bound for Luxor moved off. Cairo's station platforms, inside the vast iron structure, disappeared, and the figure of Nabila waving goodbye grew smaller.

'Write,' she said to him, and he nodded his head, smiling, for he wouldn't be away for more than four days: he was to meet the group of architects and would then return with them by plane.

Ramzi experienced a happiness whose special taste he had known as a child. He leaned his head back on the comfortable seat in the air-conditioned Upper Egypt express and looked out of the window: the outskirts of Cairo, the small old houses, the windows and balconies through which he might be given the chance of peeping in at the rites of daily life.

Nabila had a special magic. The way she acted out that he should write, pursing her lips so as to pronounce the word 'write'. Ramzi smiled.

But marriage too was a cloud that could give water or not, though in both cases it obscured the sun. And Nabila, if she wanted to, knew how to obscure the sun.

'On your return your eyes will inform me what your hands have done,' Nabila had said to him yesterday as she fondled her body with his hand. 'In Luxor there are many foreign women' – scolding him for a misdeed he had not committed.

Ramzi had seen Nabila during a visit he had made to his aunt's house.

'Nabila, the daughter of Dr Fakhri Rashad, our neighbour,' his aunt had introduced her to him.

'Glad to meet you,' Ramzi had greeted her that day, his breath caught in his chest because of his intense admiration.

'Ramzi, my nephew, an architect,' the aunt perfected the tying of the thread between buyer and seller. No sooner had his aunt left the room than Ramzi's gaze alighted on Nabila's arm, tracing that warm line that ran from the bare shoulder down to the hand, which at that instant she had raised slightly: in it she held a thread by which she was pulling that heart which had so often throbbed rapidly at such moments when the body is in command.

Ramzi sat up straight as he asked the restaurant-car attendant for a glass of tea and a packet of cigarettes. He had a sense of elation at being in this place at this time. Here he was on his way to Luxor to meet the group of American architects who had been commissioned to make a feasibility study for building the new Ahmas Hotel in a joint venture with the firm he worked for.

'A wonderful opportunity for working with this American firm,' Ramzi had said, talking to Nabila about his dreams before they materialized. 'It's a large firm and if we co-operate with them in the building of that hotel, it's not out of the question that I'll get a contract to work with them. We might go to America.' He had kept quiet for a while, then continued: 'In that event it would be possible for us to visit my nephew, Kamil Fawzi, and stay with him, because he has invited me several times.'

Nabila saw before her planes, ships and television series. 'We'll go to California,' she had answered, 'for my friend Mimi tells me it has fantastic weather.'

'We'd be going to Detroit, which is where the firm is,' Ramzi pointed out, and Nabila didn't raise any objections, because she reckoned it was quite close to California.

Ramzi smiled. Green fields stretched out and in the distance a chain of the eastern mountains came into sight. He became conscious of the sound of the attendant stirring the tea, announcing his presence. He took the packet of cigarettes and lit one. He enjoyed the first puff accompanied by a sip of tea. He saw a number of peasants working under the intense heat of the sun. He had a momentary feeling of dejection, which he lost as he thought about the sort of life he would have if he went to America.

Fakhri Rashad worked as a doctor for only three days a week so that he could devote the rest of his time to his favourite hobby, which he regarded as his real work. This was transcribing and collecting old books dealing with herbs and nature cures, the celestial bodies, and other such forgotten sciences in which what are called 'the ancients' excelled. From Sunday to Wednesday he would start his weekly journey, divided up between visiting old libraries and passing by second-hand bookstores, and in reading, sorting through, classifying, copying, checking and similar librarianship procedures on which he would spend hours and days.

'My father loves old books,' said Nabila to Ramzi when he asked her what he did, on first seeing her at his aunt's house.

He had visited her at her home to ask her father for her hand a mere week after having seen her. He had been unable to wait, with the image of her moving hand and the way she had of speaking. Dr Rashad had taken him to his place of work, or library, and had shown him a number of the transcriptions he had brought to life from timeworn and tattered pieces of paper. Ramzi also saw numerous papyri inscribed with hieroglyphics, Coptic and other such symbols, the sight of which put him in mind of museums and dusty books.

'You're Pisces – that's right for your work as an architect. Nabila has a special intelligence that relies on the essence. She doesn't like reading,' said the father, agreeing to

The Journey of Ra

their marrying.

'You read for me,' concluded Nabila, raising the shoulder that had been one of the incentives to this marriage.

'Thabit ibn Qurra did it several hundred years before us. He arranged diseases and the methods for curing them. We merely re-enact the roles.' He laughed and Ramzi felt embarrassed at such intense attempts to dazzle him.

'Thabit ibn Qurra?' Ramzi repeated, seeking by the tone of voice, an explanation from the father, while, in his mind, wholly immersed in kissing and embracing Nabila, who was aware of him and his glances penetrating through all locked doors. This is what she loved in him, and this is what made her not hesitate in asking him to meet her father.

'This is Sirius.' The father pointed to a grey-coloured dog. Ramzi had misgivings about it and retreated several paces when it came up to him to smell his trousers and shoes. 'I named him after the title of Olaf Stapledon's novel.'

Nabila went out of the room and Ramzi followed her with his eyes.

'Have you read it?'

'No, I've never heard of it.'

'He's a famous English author and one of the most important historians. I'll lend it to you if you like' – and he went to one of the bookcases that filled the room and began looking for it.

'He's a mental case,' Ramzi said to himself,

trying to hide a smile that had appeared on his face as he imagined himself in this room after the death of the father, rummaging through the books while Nabila noted down the titles preparatory to them being sold at some world auction in London or perhaps even New York.

'All these manuscripts ...!' Ramzi remarked to the father, who had come back with an elegantly bound book on the spine of which was written in gold lettering 'Dr Fakhri Rashad'.

The dog barked at the return of Nabila who, in passing through between the desk and the window, had gently touched Ramzi. He had almost laughed out loud. Nabila had a bodily presence he had not known in anyone before. 'Gazelle' – he moved his lips at Nabila without pronouncing the word. She smiled and threw back her hair, which had been lying around her neck.

Thus, in less than two weeks, the marriage had taken place of two people who had chosen to fall in love with one another.

'Isn't it a bit hasty?' the father asked them.

'No,' they answered.

And as, according to Dr Rashad's belief, most of us do not realize why it is we enter and leave by certain doors at determined times, he had agreed that the rites of marriage should be carried out.

Ever since he had met them all at Luxor Airport and seen her descending from the plane, without knowing of course that she was with the group, in fact was heading it, he had been attracted to her.

In the morning, when taking the ferry to the western bank on their way to examine certain sites chosen for the hotel building, he had learnt more from her about the history of the area than he had during his whole life, for she knew about the temples, the kings and queens, the places and dates. She even spoke a few words to him in colloquial Arabic, which she told him she had been studying because of her delight at how musical it was, also to help her in her work during the period the hotel was being built.

'No doubt you were an Egyptian in your previous life,' Ramzi told her, in delight and astonishment.

At this, Jean Miller passed her hand across the surface of the water, cleft by the passage of the ferry. She filled the palm of her hand and, with a gesture almost of supplication, brought it up to her lips and moistened them.

'He who drinks from the Nile returns to it,' she said, as though in prayer.

It was with great effort that Ramzi held himself back from embracing her and kissing that mouth that had uttered these words. He plunged his fingers caressingly into the water.

'You're a miracle, a real miracle,' sighed Ramzi, not believing what was happening around him.

In front of the balcony an Egyptian girl

wearing a *galabia* passed by. She gave them a look that brought Ramzi back from the memory of the morning to how delightful an evening it was. His gaze held hers for several moments until she had passed by.

'The Egyptian woman is fascinating and one of the most feminine,' said John Fisher as he refilled their glasses with more iced beer. 'Their way of walking and swaying their buttocks is a delight to watch.'

Ramzi smiled shyly at what this foreigner was saying so frankly about Egyptian women. He took out a packet of Marlboro cigarettes he had bought from the hotel and slowly opened it. He passed them around, then lit one for himself. He drew on it deeply and looked at the sun as it was about to sink behind the western mountains, and he remembered Nabila, or perhaps he had been reminded of her by that girl. No more than five weeks had passed since their marriage and here he was with his heart beating for this American woman.

'Are you married, Mr Fahmi?' Ramzi heard John Fisher ask him.

Disconcerted for an instant, he replied in the affirmative: 'Yes.' Then looking at Jean Miller, he added: 'Just five weeks ago.'

The two men called out jubilantly and the four glasses were refilled and the health of the new bride was drunk.

For the first time Andy Simon spoke: 'So you have little experience of that equation known as marriage.'

Ramzi did not understand the remark of

the structural engineer, who had been silent most of the time and seemed to be isolated from them. However, he smiled weakly, irritated at the exchange on this subject in front of Jean Miller.

'She must be extremely beautiful,' whispered Jean Miller, looking straight into his eyes for the first time. He didn't hear what she had said, or, if he did, it didn't register because of the look she had given him.

'You must be missing her like mad,' said John Fisher. As for Andy Simon, he appeared to be busy watching the secondary-school girls who were walking in front of the hotel and examining these foreigners on the balcony.

A cold breeze was blowing and goose pimples appeared on the arms and shoulders of Jean Miller. Under the flimsy blouse Ramzi could see the swelling breasts.

'Are you cold?' he asked her, as though he had known her for years.

'No, the weather couldn't be more beautiful,' she answered, lying back in her chair. She pointed towards the western bank where the sun was high up on the mountain:

'It's there that I want to build the hotel, where the sun is disappearing behind those mountains and will never be out of the sight of those staying there, so that Ra may not pass in his death journey of everlasting terror.'

Ramzi sensed that he was a stranger to all these ideas, although his heart almost split apart at the effect of her voice talking with such sympathy. He remembered his father-in-law, Dr Rashad, talking to him about history, about the Pharaohs, the Copts and the Arabs. But this foreigner, how did she know all this? How did she possess such sensitivity towards it? And this way she had of speaking, almost as if she were praying. Ramzi lit a cigarette from the one already in his hand.

'It won't be easy to get there,' said Ramzi, smiling, and with his eyes he kissed her whole body.

'The important thing is the sweetness of arrival.' Jean Miller gave a laugh that came from depths whose location in this volatile butterfly Ramzi was incapable of understanding.

'I shall come to meet you when you arrive.' Nabila's words of farewell came back to him. 'How I love meeting people at the airport!'

'My wife's father is a magician,' Ramzi told them. When it seemed that they were unable to understand what he meant, for his words had not met the usual attention they gave him, he went on to explain: 'He's interested in such things as astronomy, palmistry, ancient medicine and the like. He told me about many matters that astonished me.'

'Great,' said Andy, while Jean Miller lit a cigarette from Ramzi's packet.

'You, for example, must be Pisces, which is propitious for your work as an architect,' Ramzi said to Jean Miller, laughing, the beer having made its way to his head. She gave

The Journey of Ra

the same laugh he found difficult to connect with her and in which he had previously heard something that baffled him.

'I like reading too, but I adore architecture.' He began talking about himself, as his gaze followed the flow of the Nile. 'It will be a magnificent hotel on top of the mountains, where the sun is now. We studied these things at secondary school – the names of the kings, and also, at university, we turned our attention to some of the characteristics of Pharaonic architecture in the course on the history of architecture.'

Ramzi was silent for a while, then continued, addressing himself to Jean Miller, who showed the first signs of drowsiness. 'I think the sight of skyscrapers must be exceedingly exciting. How I'd love to go to America and work there! Perhaps after finishing this hotel project. The type of life is different even from Europe, many of whose capitals I have visited.'

Jean Miller awoke from a short doze to the sound of Ramzi talking about the cities he had visited. Once again she let her gaze rove across where the western mountains lay, now hidden in the darkness of night. She looked at Andy Simon, who was sunk in his contemplation of her. She seized his hand between hers for a moment, then raised it to her lips and, in that same voice that had intoxicated Ramzi, she addressed Andy Simon in a low voice: 'And because Ra must wake early tomorrow in order to make his journey to Cairo and thence to Detroit, he had better go up with me now.'

She rose to her feet. She leant her hand for an instant on Ramzi's shoulder. She patted it, then gave her other hand to Andy Simon, who dexterously clasped it under his arm. They thanked Ramzi for the lovely evening, then the two of them walked towards the swing doors separating the balcony from the hotel.

'I shan't go up to my room before finishing off another bottle,' said John Fisher to Ramzi with great relish. With a smile he added: 'Let's share it.'

4

The Thousandth Journey

On my thousandth journey into the desert I pitched my tent close to a spring belonging to some bedouin I had known since my childhood. On a semi-moonlit night I went up the gentle slope of the mountain till I came to a circular place from where I could see the valley. I gazed at the distant stars for a while, after which I went down to Hasan al-Qureishi, the Sheikh of the tribe and my spiritual guide. He was at the time drinking tea in front of his tent. It is to him I have recourse when my soul yearns for its unique origin.

'Free me today,' I said to him. He was always promising to free me to the utmost limit, so long as I had no fear, that my vision did not stray and that I was not scared by fantasies.

'Let us wait two nights and on the third I shall free you,' he informed me, as was his wont each time. Smiling, he showed his broken teeth and a tongue cracked by dryness.

On the third night I went to him that he might carry out his promise. When he saw me he asked me how much water I had drunk and I answered him, and what was the most recent food I had eaten and I informed him.

He shook his head disapprovingly: 'Bully-beef?' He laughed and gave me some dried dates. He advised me to go on living in solitude in my place on the mountain and to bathe at dawn and in the evening.

He struck the ground with his hand and brought forth a beetle. He handed it to me and enjoined me to commune with it during my period of solitude, until the time for making my departure.

From on top of the mountain, within the circle assigned to be by my Sheikh, I went on following the beetle wherever it went, and when it had almost disappeared I would bring it back to my side. I did not sleep lest it make its escape, and not for an instant did I take my eyes off it.

'O lovely beetle, you will spend only one more night away from home and then I shall return you to your children, and to your husband or wife. Do not be in such a panic. Through you my soul may be liberated from the desire for the perception of a divine secret which, without you, it is not within my capacity to attain.'

It never conversed with me and paid no attention. All that concerned it was to run away and escape.

On the third night I returned to the Sheikh, together with the gift he had made me. He planted it back in the ground from where he had extracted it and asked me: 'Did you eat the dates?'

'All of them.'

'And it?'

'What?'

'The beetle.'

'Does it eat dates?'

'Do I leave it with you for you to deprive it and starve it? You will have no release unless you compensate for that.'

'As you say.'

Sheikh Hasan gave his suppressed laugh and with his body leaned across a nearby rock and produced a mouse, which he gently held out to me. When signs of fear and disgust showed on my face, he turned his head away, with his hand still outstretched, so I took it. He made me promise to show it affection, also a willingness to comply with its wishes, and not to deprive it of food – and he supplied me with a small piece of bread and a cupful of milk.

Enclosing it in the palm of my hand, I returned to my place. I could feel it trying to slip out as it attempted to gnaw at my timorous fingers. I did not dare to allow it its freedom as it might dart away from me. I grasped hold of it and asked it to be kind to me, for it was the instrument of my release. With one hand I started to crumble the bread for it, and while it lay under my other hand I brought some crumbs close up to it, but it would not eat. All it did was to struggle frantically to escape.

I put the milk down for it, having denied myself, for I would not drink of it should it have tasted it. It sniffed at it but abstained, thus depriving me, though without itself having drunk.

On the third night I was tortured by drowsiness, so I decided to dig a hollow of a suitable size and to place it there, shielding it with my chest and praying that it might not escape. Its head and whiskers tormented me and I was upset by the swinging motion of its tail. Eventually I dozed off. At dawn I found it a lifeless corpse. Sorrowfully, I buried it and returned to my Sheikh and recounted my story to him. He frowned and mumbled to himself. I sensed that he was on the point of dismissing me, for I had starved the beetle and stifled the mouse. And now?

'And now?' I asked him.

'Do you still wish to be freed?'

'Forgive me, for I am a city-dweller and have no such know-how.'

'Never mind,' he said to me, for he loved me dearly. He got up and came back with a gecko, or perhaps it was a chameleon, twice the size of the mouse, with five fingers ending in circular pads.

'Take it and take care of it. Don't let it infatuate you and don't slay it. It will not run away and it has eaten its fill for months to come. Gather it up to yourself, enjoy its company, and may you be successful. Don't talk too little or too much with it.'

He handed over my food to me and bade me farewell.

I took it and clasped it to my breast. It submitted and put up no resistance.

I went back to my place. I saw its eyes regarding me and it stuck out its tongue and conversed with me. I implored it to be nice to me, for there is no assurance about life. It deliberated with me with the softness of its belly and tormented me with friction. I said to myself: 'Let me try.' I released it in front of me, I its supervisor and custodian. It crouched where it was in front of me, observing me while I watched over it.

On the fourth night my spiritual guide came to me, for he had realized the reason for my delay.

'It has induced forgetfulness in you, and your destiny has been lost to you.' He chased it away and it took shelter in the rocks. I came to with water being sprinkled on my face, and he brought me back to where his tent was, to the date palm and the spring of water.

'I did my best.'

'Listen to what I say.'

'I bore in mind all you said, but it did not stop looking and talking.'

'I shall not try out the fox and the wolf and the hyena, the cat and the leopard and the lion. Not many nights remain before the waning of the moon. I have great affection for you, and so I shall make an attempt with you for the thousandth time,' he said to me, smiling or in despair.

He entered his tent and came out with a young girl and a goat. He looked at me and made me swear to treat them kindly, for, on the third and last night, if I was not cured of the deviation of my soul, there would be no way in which I would be freed.

I returned to my place and began talking to the young girl about appropriate matters: the names of the mountains and the stars, the attributes of imagination, and of male and female camels.

She was like a gazelle. Her name was Na'ila, Na'ila the daughter of Hasan.

On the first evening she sat and milked the goat and intoxicated me with the crescent moon.

On the second morning she woke me with a date sweet as honey in my mouth. On the same night she named the stars for me, sang some melodies, and, claiming she was a wolf, gave me a fright. Then she patted me on the shoulder and put me to sleep like a doll in her lap. She removed fear from me by telling me that she herself was the wolf: 'There is no one on the mountain except Na'ila, you and the goat.'

On the third day at noon, the heat having become intense, she advised me to discard my clothes and massaged my burning body with pure milk.

In the evening she roamed about me in imagination. When we were well into the night, she removed my confusion through proximity and completed her education of me by elucidating the parts of the body: here is the nose, here the neck, this is called a breast, that the navel, then the fist, the upper arm, the belly, the white and black of the eye, the eyelashes, the palm of the hand, the foot, the stomach and the vulva – and she pointed to the genitals and I had a vision of bed, then she touched the eyebrow and asked me about frottage and intercourse with penetration.

On the third night I returned and talked to him.

'What happened with her?'

'God knows that I did not stretch out my hand, nor act wrongly towards my Sheikh, nor seek gratification for myself in seclusion.'

'I know, I know. However, I am referring to the goat.'

'The goat? The goat?'

I was lost for words, for it was as though there had never been a goat. For an instant I was detained by the vision of it as it looked at me while Na'ila was drawing off the milk I had drunk and with which I had been massaged.

I knew that the time for my return had drawn near and in this journey, too, I had missed the chance of release.

5

The Rivalry

A clearly defined goal took possession of Abu'l-Sulouk of Cordoba. It seemed to him that in the knowledge of the laws of light and shadow lies a primary essence through which can be revealed the true nature of possibilities. In conformity with it someone who wishes to be conveyed between different places, can fly; or his personality can become distributed in two individuals with separate bodies; likewise, he can disappear from sight or make an appearance.

With the passing of the years he became more determined to discover the dimensions of proofs. Every night he would go to his laboratory adjoining his house, where he would find that his faithful assistant and student, Dawn-Lights, had made ready the experimental equipment: the stick and two wooden balls, the candle and the pigeon which he had trained to spread its wings at different angles according to the appointed times of the moon observed from a top window.

But tonight was not like every night, for tomorrow he had his appointment with the calligrapher Abu'l-Sanad of Ghazna, the final appointment to which each would bring what he had finally accomplished in respect of the origin of the primary essence.

As for today, here at last he was convinced of attaining his objective and of completing what he had begun or, to be more exact, of perfecting what al-Bariq of Seville, Mushi' of Toledo and Jinah al-Kurki of Qaft had striven to do before him.

'If you were able,' he went on telling himself the whole day long – 'if you were successful in kneading together light with shadow, and in bending the line of rays, there would thereafter be no problem too difficult for you and you would need no interpretation. In fact I shall go to him, the leader of dissemblers, the expert on corruption and fraud, Abu'l-Sanad of Ghazna. I shall fly over his head, the pasturage of the levels of ignorance, and above him I shall sit, without his touch defiling me, so as to prove to him the validity of my conjecture and the significance of all these years I have spent in accumulating and examining. And in the spectacle of me being suspended in the air without chair or hoop will be a vindication of my theory, a spur to his returning to the truth, and a deliverance for the naïve souls who jostle at his door every day, yearning to grasp his fallacious concept, poison enveloped in honey: that in the letter and number, dot and line, is the primary essence by which the knot of ignorance is untied, also by which the mirror of cognitive subtleties is polished. In conformity with it someone can fly who wants to be conveyed between places, or to two individuals, his personality being differently distributed within two bodies; likewise he can disappear from sight or make an appearance.

In the middle of the room stood Dawn-Lights awaiting his master, conscious of the extent of the importance of this night. With every step the master was taking, his heartbeats were increasing in terror: What if he were to fail? Had he not tested the shadow of the candle? The shadow of the moon? The shadow of the fire? Had they not even taken the stick, the two balls, and the pigeon hidden within his cloak, outside the city walls? He would let it fly and it wouldn't fly. As for him, he would not rise, not so much as a finger's breadth, from the ground.

'Not by a mere finger's breadth did he rise.'

The importance of the night made the thoughts in Dawn-Lights' head chase after one another. 'If my master fails, there is no way for it but to take that step that has been tempting me during the long time I have been tortured by anxiety: there is no way but to take Abu'l-Sanad as a master instead of Abu'l-Sulouk.'

But how, after the elapse of all these years, having been the faithful disciple of his master, who had even chosen for him his name Dawn-Lights, how could he betray him by becoming a follower of his one and only rival? So he would say, following the method of his empirical master: 'The years have passed and life is fleeing, and maybe the number and the letter, the dot and the line, are more suited to my temperament, irrespective of gains or preternatural phenomena. All I wish for is to be closely associated with a master who loves me and whom I love.'

It was as though fate were making fun of the confusion of mankind. On all these occasions when his master had failed, on all these occasions Word-Secret, the student and deputy of Abu'l-Sanad, would come to him from he knew not where, appearing to him suddenly whilst he was sitting at the café. Word-Secret would take a place alongside him and would ease his sadness by story-telling, by chatting and recounting anecdotes, so that he would draw him away, soaring off behind him into worlds and sensations that excite the emotions or feed the imagination.

After each of these times how often would he console himself and turn his mind away from doubt, for sensations, the products of imagination, are more deeply embedded in the spirit that those arising from thought.

'Tonight – the last night, O Lights.' Dawn-Lights awoke to the voice of his master.

'Have you the equipment ready?' Before he answered him, Abu'l-Sulouk had gone to

The Rivalry

the cage in the corner of the room and had taken out the pigeon which, from much training, had become used to its work, performing it without fear of punishment or hope of approval. Dawn-Lights hurried along behind the teacher with the candle, the stick and the two balls. Below the high window Abu'l-Sulouk sat down, the stick in his hand, and the two balls underneath the wings of the pigeon.

It tried to rise without avail.

The moon looked down upon them and everyone's shadow danced upon the walls.

At the very same time, Abu'l-Sanad was placing letter above letter, and the dot and the line, in the courtyard of his house in expectancy of the miracle, and his deputy Word-Secret was keeping at bay the people gathered at his door. Word-Secret took delight in talking of him, praising his uniqueness, and mixing love with yearning. He would utter the words clearly, would then hum them, then chant them, then invert them, then repeat them in full after apocopating them.

Whenever the crowd lost their senses and understanding, he would vanish from their sight without their realizing whether he was among them or had disappeared. He would hurry towards him who had taught him and would find, time and time again, that he was still in his chair.

6

Lover-Narrator

On the outskirts of a city a man set up an orphanage; in fact it was more of a school or small factory than an orphanage. Its wares were the abilities of the orphan boys, developed from early youth by the owner of the place. On the arrival of a fresh newcomer, the man would prepare him for one of the jobs he would later earn money from.

Among the boys being trained was the Reckoner, who had a flare for the fundamentals of the sciences of adding and subtracting, multiplying and dividing, and solving equations. His task was to organize the work of large stores. The Genealogist was he who had learnt by heart the genealogies of the leading members of the families of the district and the relationships of family trees. There were also among them boys possessed of strong bodies and courage, like the Smasher, the Battler, the Hailer and the Goader.

The remarkable genius of the owner of the orphanage lay in distributing the futures of the children. Thus the Reckoner had to be possessed, in his bodily make-up, of a large head, narrow eyes, a broad back to his neck and long fingers. Thus, too, for example, the Chatterer, who was admirable at talking, story-telling and singing, and was hired out for parties, was distinguished by a wide mouth, large ears and a fat bottom. Then there was the Supplicator to whom everyone with a request would resort, be he seeking good or intending evil; he was an expert in matters of mediation, conversant with souls and their spirits, with the names of the angels of the *djinn*, and was capable of calling upon the uppermost heavens and placating the nethermost places; from early youth he was distinguished by a roundness of face, a delicate nose and smallness of stature, also perhaps by a difficulty in articulation or hearing. Among these special types was the Cipherer, the solver of ciphers, and the Inflator with the broad chest, who was capable of drawing in enormous quantities of air, either hot or cold. There was the Fighter, who was always in demand and in respect of whom the owner of the orphanage never suffered a loss in spending on him. There was also the Howler, who was good at wailing and versed in the inmost secrets of souls, where and when to stir them. And there was also the Accoucheur and the Interrer and the *Kohl*-Applier and the Builder and the Demolisher and the Watcher and the Healer

Lover-Narrator

and the Envier and the Effacer and the Bringer-together-in-love.

There spoke to us Genealogist the genealogist, who knows the dates and genealogies of the whole city, its past and its present, and has also committed to mind the life histories of the persons of distinction and is conversant with strange and wonderful stories and has memorized a thousand books. He was the last of the genealogists at the orphanage set up by Amin Bey al-Sahrawalti, the last of the line of al-Sahrawalti, who was killed by some of the orphans who were greedy for clay jars filled with gold that he was hiding.

Said Genealogist – this being his name and surname – recounting in full the story whose episodes had taken place more than half a century ago, there being no longer any danger for those who had participated in it, they having passed into oblivion and departed from this place, be it by having travelled away or by having died:

'I am Genealogist, this being my name and surname. Our master, Amin Bey – and at that time we used to call him our master in that he was our benefactor – was in the habit of calling us according to our jobs. After he had got hold of us by having come across our bodies abandoned on the steps of places of worship or in dark alleyways, or after our parents had disappeared, having left us in front of his orphanage, or had even handed us over to him, he used to choose a future or name for each of us, and this would stick to us until we died. How astonished I was, with me being the memorizer of his history, and of the history of those who were before me, at how perspicacious and unerring in his judgement he was! Only in two instances was he forced to change destinies: the first was the case of Grabber, who gave the impression from early youth of having extraordinary strength in his hand-clasp, though after the age of about seven he changed to Eulogist. In the same way he changed Battler to Poet. Even in these two rare instances there was in his original choice a certain sagacity, and there remained in both Eulogist and Poet traces of their first destiny.

'At that time we were the dependants of Amin Bey; we would work for a wage which we would hand over to him, each one according to his job, while he would look after our needs in the matter of food, clothes and the necessities of life.

'He used – may God have mercy upon him – to give each one his due. Though our wages differed, yet he would treat us equally. He would nevertheless, for reasons best known to himself, differentiate between us in the type of food and the quantity. Thus he would give the Battler lots of meat, the Supplicator lots of fish, and the Cipherer lots of spinach, and so on. Due to the different natures of individuals, this was often the cause of resentment. I would include myself among them owing to the fact that, though still being a boy in those days, I used to love piquant and tasty foods and was forbidden them on the pretext that they enfeebled the memory upon which my job depended. Because of the differing natures of human beings, the orphans would often attempt, sometimes by entreaty, sometimes by having someone intercede for them, and sometimes even by slipping off at night to the kitchen, they would attempt – though without avail – to change their prescribed diets. This was because, though indulgent and generous – may God have mercy upon him – he was in this respect both strict and unyielding.

'During this period we came to know another truth of which we had been ignorant. One night Supplicator came to us after Amin Bey had gone off home, our rooms being separated from his home by a spacious garden ending in a high wall. We had never seen what lay behind it, although I memorized from the genealogists who were there before me that "Amin Bey al-Sahrawalti had a magnificent dwelling lying behind the high wall which was at the end of the spacious garden that stood in front of the orphans' rooms."

'On that night, after Amin Bey had disappeared, and we always had our doubts about him in that he would be with us and all of a sudden wouldn't be; how many days and nights we spent thinking he was watching us, or keeping watch over us, only to discover after the passage of time that he had travelled away to relax . . .

'On that night, sixty-six full years, three

months and twelve days ago, while we were gathered in the spacious dining room, each one eating what had been allocated to him, Supplicator began – having completed working the whole of the day, he being one of those most sought after for work – Supplicator began whispering in our ears that piece of knowledge which was later to change the history of us all. It was this piece of news that was embellished for the group of Cosmeticians and for one of the Builders, who kept dreaming of executing a new building for the orphans, a building superior to any palaces previously built, and also for one of the Cleavers, who was the most famed for ripping open animals and cleaving the skin, and finally for Lover-Narrator, who in truth was nothing more than a narrator who was an expert in pronouncing languages, entertaining people and making them laugh, but who was nicknamed amongst us as Lover because of his love for our lady of the beauty-spot, the wife of our master, whom we had never seen but about whom I had memorized from the history of genealogies that she was Huda Hanim, the daughter of Ibrahim Bey, owner of businesses in East and West and the first to introduce garments of gold and silver thread, and at whose hands the Singer, the Author, the Eulogist, the Applauder and the Toastmaster had become famous. She was the first woman to have a beauty-spot appear above her lips, and thus she was known as 'the lady of the beauty-spot'. When she walked, forty-three tyres of fat danced behind her, and when she sat down twenty-one folds supported her. When she cast a glance, the heart of the immune melted, and when she laughed, he whose heart was as hard as stone, softened. She was expert in the skills of dancing, singing and playing musical instruments; and it was she who was in absolute command when inspiring love, she who was shielding that hidden star for whose sake the lives of numerous lovers had been wiped out.'

Genealogist stopped, then concluded, having remembered what had passed ages and ages ago:

'The last of them was Lover-Narrator, who had not tasted sleep since that time he was entertaining a party of the town's eminent personalities in an assembly of men and women. Suddenly, like lightning striking after dazzling the eye, there had entered upon them a woman who, no sooner did she sit down amongst them, than there was diffused the aroma of sweet musk; and who, no sooner did she open her mouth, than words sweet as honey issued forth; and who, no sooner did she cast a glance, than a union of hearts was formed. Lover-Narrator was in the spring of his life, as yet a virgin. As for this woman, she would sometimes commence to speak and would then become silent, would stand up and then sit down, would dance and then weep, be lost in thought and then come to, and finally would withdraw like a breeze fragrant with love's yearning. After she had disappeared from the sight of those present, they remained like people hypnotized, until they regained consciousness and found themselves mentioning her name and discussing her: the most famous and most beautiful woman on earth, my lady of the beauty-spot.

'Thereafter Lover-Narrator knew no peace; his body was no longer able to relax, nor did his imagination rest at night for journeying in remembrance of her, of how she sat, of how she cast a glance, of how she behaved in her every movement. He kept it secret and told not a living soul that he had seen the wife of Amin Bey. When, later on, he talked and muddled things up and little bits and pieces found their way into his conversation, he would utter her name, the name of the person who had changed the course of his life and who, according to his own words, had driven away the long night. Whenever he mentioned her name, she whom he had named "Morn", he wept.

'Let us return to the purport of our story and how it was that Amin Bey, the last of the owners of the orphanage, met his end, and how it was that Huda Hanim, the lady of the beauty-spot, Lover-Narrator's Morn, was killed the same night.

'One night many years ago we were as usual gathered in the dining room at a late hour. All the orphans of the home had returned, both those of us who had been working all day, either outside or inside, also those who had spent their day in learning by heart or in practice or implementation. Each one ate what was prescribed or destined for him. So the group that took part in that crime came together, after having assumed that Amin Bey had disappeared as usual and having confirmed that he was not watching them. On that night sixty-six years, three months and twelve days ago, and while the orphans were gathered in the spacious dining hall, Supplicator began whispering in our ears that bit of knowledge, or aggregate of knowledge, that jostled on his tongue. During his work that day at the house of a woman from an old and respectable family having ancient and strong ties with Amin Bey's family, she had asked him to pray for the deaths of two people, once for Huda Hanim's death because she had been responsible for her eldest son losing his senses ever since he had seen her just the once at a gathering of certain notables, when she had stood up and sat down, and wept and danced. She had also asked for the death of Amin Bey, stealer of children and slave-trader, because he had seduced her and had stayed for years and years feeding off her love and passion for him, and now it was his intention, having hidden away the gold in jars, to elope with a new woman.

'On that night the oath was taken to perpetrate the crime. The first to do so was the group of Cosmeticians. The reason for their hatred of our master was that the food allocated to them consisted merely of boiled vegetables, so that they might be nimble and of slender physique for carrying out those of their tasks which were arduous such as embrocation, scrubbing and massaging, without overtiring the clients. Also, the story of the jars filled with gold had created for them visions of laying their hands on enough to be able to flee to independence from that prison.

'Builder likewise – without hesitation, for this was his dream – took part: to do away with our master who would never give him the chance of completing the ideal building he imagined for orphans and for the accomplishment of which he had to have a jar or two.

'As for Cleaver, he had taken the oath because of his great fear of the poverty that might befall him were our master to give up the orphanage, having become used to the best of meat and drink. As his job required phenomenal strength, Amin Bey did not stint him where meat broth and fatty foods were concerned. Additionally, he had learnt from our master not to waste any opportunity that might come to him in his professional life in the way of new experience in the fields of ripping and cleaving.

'As for Lover-Narrator, he was not with us at table, being still segregated as a punishment in the hope that he would come to his senses. But, having taken the oath, this group found that there was something to be gained from uniting him with themselves and using him, without his knowledge, in furthering their task.

'The plan was to lure Amin Bey to Lover-Narrator's cell, which was isolated from the rest of the orphans' rooms.

'Supplicator would first of all speak to him and inform him that Lover-Narrator had repented and had become reasonable again and that he no longer talked about Morn and would like to see his master and benefactor in order to ask his pardon. Supplicator would plead with Amin Bey to accompany him on a visit to Lover-Narrator so that he could confirm things for himself. During this visit the cosmetic group would distract the rest of the orphans, who for the most part worshipped our benefactor, sometimes by deception, sometimes by massage and embrocation, so that they gained their attention. Then the Builder would join up with the Cleaver to accomplish the task. They would do away with Amin Bey and take possession of the keys to his house.

'In this way they devised the plan by making use of Lover-Narrator, by telling him that Amin Bey was the husband of Morn, a woman they believed to be an invention of his madness. They told him that if they did away with Amin Bey and got possession of the keys, the way would be free for him to carry out his lifelong dream and ambition of seeing her; in fact they even promised him that he would have his way with her if he were to help them.

'Thus on the first night on which our master remained with us until suppertime without disappearing, Supplicator, the orphan closest to his heart, approached him and informed him about Lover-Narrator having come to his senses.

'After the completion of the crime in its every detail, and after the orphans had gone to sleep, they burst into the house, each one proceeding on his way: Lover-Narrator to the bedchamber of his Morn of the beauty-spot, and the rest of them to Amin Bey's room so as to lay hands on the gold. After they had rifled the pots one by one, each taking his share, Supplicator went up to the bedroom of the lady so as to assure himself that the prayer requested of him had been answered. And so he found Lover-Narrator, his lips pressed to those of Morn and with his finger fondling the beauty-spot above her mouth – and her having departed this life.'

7

The Miracle

Dr Nazeer decided to pay a visit to the St Demetrios monastery in the Doum Oasis. For several days before the trip Nazeer made preparations: coloured films, a tape-recorder, white clothes suitable for the intense heat of the desert, and a fur overcoat for the cold nights. He read several books about the history of the monasteries, the martyrs and the saints. He visited a relative of his who worked at the Ministry of Land Reclamation and obtained certain information from him about the area, the roads for getting there and back, and the most favourable days for undertaking the journey. 'The trip takes approximately three days. The car stops the first night at the Sugarcane Resthouse. Don't expect too much, because all it's got is a storage tank for petrol and another one for water, linked by a small café. You'll not find any sugarcane there. Then for the second night there's the filling station from where the new road leading to the reclamation project branches off. Before noon on the third day you'll arrive at the monastery.'

And so it came about. On the third day before noon there came into view in the distance a green smudge like a small oasis, in the centre of which was a building with high walls, like some ocean-going vessel braced by the hawsers of the shadows of date palms.

At the monastery gate there were a number of priests dressed in black awaiting him, and in a spacious room with columns decorated with ivory and with gilded icons depicting male and female saints, one of the priests knelt down in front of him and washed his feet. A monk with a snow-white beard reaching down to his waist came up to him and kissed him on the left cheek, at which Nazeer gave him his right cheek and followed him.

They went by way of a long open gallery on both sides of which were a number of monastic cells like small enclosed rooms, and he was conscious of several eyes watching him from behind narrow apertures.

Outside the desert stretched away. The tracks of the car that had brought him had disappeared and all that remained were ridges of earth being pushed by a light wind towards the wadi.

Then there was the garden with the fig, olive and doum trees, bounded by a demarcation line of yellow sand that rose up from the direction of the tower, where the

The Miracle

wind was blowing. The palm trees shook and let fall several dates. A cock crowed once, and he turned towards the sound but made out no sign of life. The same cock or another one crowed a second time and a third, and he did not turn round. Before them there appeared momentarily a horse, an ox, a snake, a hawk, a lamb and a human being, and, when he looked closely, the horse and the snake were interjoined into a valiant lion.

The monk opened a small doorway in an extremely high gate. They descended four steps. In the centre was a coffin gilded with pictures and symbols. The monk lighted a lamp that stood on an altar. Nazeer became aware of the extent of the place; all the walls, with the exception of the gate, were shadowless. Looking up at the ceiling, he saw stars and constellations, single and in clusters. He made out Sagittarius with his bow, and he knelt down alongside the monk.

To the questions of certain relatives, friends, doctors, scientific researchers and journalists, Nazeer replied:

'A mixture of desire for knowledge and curiosity, but also an inner drive whose true nature I don't know.'

'My studies abroad did not relate directly to this subject, my thesis being on liquid mechanics.'

'Certain relatives and friends, but this was not the incentive.'

'My mother travelled away with her husband after the death of my father.'

'I am unable to answer that question.'

'I believe that many of these matters have scientific explanations, though as of now we may not know them.'

'Very few visitors; they are almost completely isolated.'

'I don't believe it was merely an accident, or fate as you would say.'

'The journey took three days.'

'My studies related to liquid mechanics, but my most important research was in the application of the second law of thermodynamics to the circulation of the blood, especially when there has been a haemorrhage.'

'My visit lasted nine days. The ninth day was the date for my return, and it was at dawn on that day that it happened. Then the car came and the journey took three days. The period in all was a fortnight.'

'It's conceivable.'

'That's what I heard from my uncle when I wanted to marry one of my fellow students abroad. He sent me a letter in which he said: "Don't marry the foreigner woman – it's enough that you killed your father." '

'Maybe.'

'How is it possible for me now to give any clear scientific answers?'

'The coffin was not completely closed; the lid was slightly open on the side facing us, open enough to allow a hand to pass through.'

The Miracle

'The light was faint, though I was not able to make out any prop on which the lid might have been resting.'

'There was no smell of putrefaction.'

'Maybe some incense, I don't know what sort.'

'One of the pious fathers, a man of miracles.'

'This is what the monk told me.'

'At least half a century.'

'Yes, I was completely conscious.'

'He asked me if I had any questions I wanted the answer to, or any request, wish or the like.'

'I stretched out my right hand through the opening between the lid and the coffin, and, as he told me to do, I touched the nearby part where the head was.'

'I was not able to see anything inside, but I am certain that it was not a living human being.'

'The feeling was similar to touching a body that has recently died. It reminded me of my initial days of study in the dissecting hall of the College of Medicine.'

'Yes, I undertook my engineering studies after completing my study of medicine.'

'I asked about who had killed my father – that is if he *was* killed.'

'There was no pain. No, I didn't feel any pain, and there was no bleeding.'

'He did not exactly warn me, though he enjoined me to be sincere with myself.'

'And how was I to know?'

'I have no doubts about that theory. This

would only be possible in the event of a wound.'
'That's what I am unable to explain.'
'Impossible. He was praying at the time in front of an icon close to the gate.'
'Neither the edge of the coffin nor the lid was at all jagged.'
'Maybe.'
'Naturally, solely my responsibility.'
'The whole of my arm, right up to the shoulder, was inside.'
'I was thinking about whether my father had died from being poisoned.'
'Yes, I know.'
'I am unable to answer that question.'
'I don't accuse anyone.'
'Perhaps that was the price of knowledge.'
'I have previously answered that question. I have my doubts about that theory. This might be possible in the event of a wound but not in that of amputation.'

8

The Slave's Dream

Close by one of the Pyramids a friend of mine had built himself a small house to which he would go to escape from the clamour of the city. Generally he would be accompanied by his wife and their only daughter and they would spend the weekend in the peace of the desert.

After having made excuses several times, I was persuaded by his saying 'It's only an hour away and you'll find yourself in another world.'

The sands stretched out and I marvelled at his perseverance in cultivating the small garden. The view of the Pyramid from so near was magnificent. Knowing as he did my dislike of being cut off from life, he began enumerating to me the merits of the place: the clean air, the peace of mind, the fresh vegetables he had succeeded in getting established after repeated efforts. He explained to me how he had sunk the well, about the alluvial mud he had transported there, and the crop rotations. His wife busied herself seasoning our supper with some of the various herbs that their land under cultivation presented them with and which had been gathered by their daughter.

It was before eight o'clock that he took me to my room by the light of a kerosene lamp, promising me a splendid dawn: 'We sleep early so as to wake early.'

Through a small window the sky showed clear and filled with stars. I tried to read a while by the faint light but the cold and the bareness of the place prevented me. I gave myself up to the bed and wished for sleep.

I don't know how much time had passed except that I well remember the sound of the scream. At first I imagined it was a dream, but the screaming went on and led me to go into the small hallway that separated their room from mine. The first thing that occurred was that I received a hard blow to the face that felled me. A man sprang on me and bound my hands behind my back, while another pointed a gun at my head; a third was delivering kicks at my friend and a fourth was struggling with the wife as he forced her outside. I didn't see the daughter though I could hear her screaming coming from the direction of the garden. With the speed of time I was pushed along, led by the muzzle of the gun, walking and falling, to the front door and out to the darkness of a car. I was thrown to the ground and heavy feet trampled on me; the word 'death' was on their lips.

The Slave's Dream

In a mountain cave, whose whereabouts I did not know, I recovered consciousness. I saw the two of them in front of me: a leper whose body was full of suppurating sores, while the second had his face eaten away by the disease, only a single eye and a twisted mouth remaining. I was aghast at the sight and in terror of my life. One of them approached me and, untying my feet, ordered me to follow him. I walked behind him to the cave entrance, where at first the light startled me. After a while I was able to see the sea, an extended range of mountains and a bare sea-shore.

Still inside the cave's gallery, he ordered me to go down and gather firewood and to return before nightfall. He made me understand that he had paid a sum of money for me to some brigands. He had bought me as a slave for the rest of my life, a slave for him and the other leper and for a group whose names he mentioned to me. 'Don't try to escape' – and from his tone of voice I believed him.

The memory of my last night with my friend, his wife and daughter came back to me. There was no point in regretting anything. Thoughts jostled in my head: Dead? Dead? Maybe escape was a possibility? What direction should I take? I would put a distance between me and them and then climb the mountain. It must be the eastern desert and the Red Sea. After the mountains there would be the valley. But without water or food? Perhaps it would be best to return to them? Perhaps I could manage it after recovering my strength? Or was it better to die now? I collected some dry branches and pieces of wood thrown up by the sea. Before nightfall I returned.

Around a fire made of the wood I had collected they were seated. From a far corner which they had defined as my territory, I saw them cooking what appeared to me to be an infant child. When they had eaten their fill, they threw me the bones that remained. On the residual coals they heated iron skewers. One of the lepers called to me and ordered me to cauterize his leprous sores, threatening to strangle me if I did not obey. He took off his clothes and stretched out on the ground. I grasped the red-hot iron in his rags to burn the body, at which the yellow liquid poured out, while the man screamed from the pain and the pleasure at one and the same time.

I spent with them several months, each day collecting firewood for them. They then revealed to me where the spring was from which they got their water and I would carry it to them on my back whenever their waterskins ran out. At night I would cauterize or lance their festering sores.

Every now and again a trader would pay them a visit and I would hear them discussing among themselves what they should barter with him. When he came they would thrust me into the dark recesses of a pit from which I was unable to climb and from which they would then pull me out. They would exchange for gold the carcases of slaughtered animals, the wine and the women that he brought them.

When he brought them a woman I would hear them all taking their pleasure with her. I was able to distinguish their several voices, for I knew by now their rasping moans, their coughs and soft sighings. She would die, or they would kill her, or they would throw her on to the pointed rocks, or they would eat her.

Often I would imagine myself escaping. I would dream about flying. Memories of my previous life would come to me. Meanwhile these painful festering sores were spreading all over my body. They would burn me whenever the firewood came into contact with them; whenever they came close to the flames, these little sacks of pus yearned to be cauterized. Drawing water from my body, they gradually swelled up and suppurated. From the pain I would rip them open on the jagged tips of rocks so that the matter – yellow, red and black – might flow out.

I want to flee, to walk the whole length of the mountains, but my swollen feet and toes no longer look the same shape. I dream of swimming yet it is enough for me to feel the sea spray for me to flee back to them.

Sometimes I grasp a stone in my hand and rend the festering sores, and my soul craves for the time when they will have pity on me, when they will take me into their company and I can eat meat and drink wine and take my pleasure with women.

Night after night I dream of the coming of the new slave.

9

The Visit

Mamdouh woke in alarm to a knocking at the door. It was not yet eight by his watch and he was not in the habit of getting up before Umm Fathi the servant arrived around ten. Mamdouh worked at night as the accounts manager of one of Cairo's large hotels, preferring solitude and quiet and avoiding the bustle of life and strong attachments which would require of him to work mornings and so have his evenings free for staying up late and going out.

Since the death of his wife a long time ago he had confined himself to his work, spending on it the greater part of his evenings and nights. His days he would pass at home in his flat, reading or just resting and relaxing.

In front of the door of the flat that early morning there stood a foreign girl of medium height carrying on her back a vast pack. The first things Mamdouh noticed about her were her dirty fingers and worn-out sandals. She was holding a map of Cairo and had circled in red the crossroads in the area where lay the building in which he lived.

'Mr Mamdouh Kamal?' the girl asked him in English in a subdued, tentative voice. Not particularly beautiful, she looked, standing there before him, like a large child weighed down by a load that was too big for her. At first Mamdouh had the impression he was at the hotel, for such a sight was all too common there – but here, at the door of his flat! Who could this girl be who knew his name and address?

In a tone tinged with annoyance and disquiet Mamdouh answered her:

'Yes, Mamdouh Kamal. Who are you?'

'I've come from Australia and I've been visiting the temples of Upper Egypt and Abu Simbel. I've seen many fascinating places in Egypt.'

This was not what he had meant, it was not an answer to his question.

Signs of having relaxed showing on her face, the girl now began to lower the heavy pack from her back after having carefully folded the map and put it in the pocket of her dress. When she lost her balance and nearly fell, Mamdouh was obliged to help her.

From early morning it had been hot and her face was running with sweat. Mamdouh noticed the red marks left by the straps on her plump shoulders.

Freed of her heavy load, the girl looked at him and asked amiably: 'Do you think you

The Visit

could let me have a glass of water, I'm absolutely dying of thirst.'

One of the neighbours, on his way to work, passed by and greeted Mamdouh, without concealing his astonishment at what he saw. In order to avoid further embarrassment at such an hour when the stairs of the building were crowded with residents and people selling things, he was forced to invite her in.

He preceded her, making no attempt to assist her with carrying her luggage. He went towards the kitchen and filled her a glass of iced water. On his return he found she had entered and brought in her pack and, having closed the door behind her, was waiting by the table in the middle of the hall. Mamdouh placed the glass of water in front of her. She drank it down, then looked at him ingratiatingly after having wiped her moist lips with the back of her hand.

'Your flat's really delightful, Mr Mamdouh.'

'Who are you?' Mamdouh asked her, this time clearly and decisively, enunciating each word. 'And from where do you know me?'

The girl sat down in a chair. She looked tired. Before answering his question she took a letter from one of the pockets of her pack and handed it to him.

He read his name and address on the envelope. He opened it hastily to find out about this strange visit. Inside he found a postcard showing the picture of a beautiful beach with trees and in the middle of them a number of small but elegant houses. He turned over the card and read:

'Dear Mamdouh,
We are writing to you from Blue Paradise where we have been living for fifteen years. We send our greetings and love through our daughter Philippa. We naturally wish you were with us.
Margaret and Michael Magoo'

At the top of the card was printed the name of the place: Blue Paradise – Australia.

Mamdouh turned over the card twice, then placed it on the table and sat down facing the girl.

Margaret and Michael Magoo. This then was their daughter who, fifteen years ago, he had seen for the last time when she was four years old – and here she was sitting in front of him. He pictured her as she used to play amongst them. He pictured too his wife Nahid, with all of them spending their summers in Alexandria before Michael was transferred to Australia.

Her father had called her Philippa because of his wish to have a boy.

Mamdouh remembered back: at that time Michael was a director of the bank in which he was working. At forty-five he had been full of health and energy, charming the women with his good looks and blond hair. On the beach at Stanley, where he had his cabin, how the women, bowled over by his physical charm, sought to attract him! Even

The Visit

Nahid would express her admiration for him. Those were the days of the past.

So this was Philippa sitting in front of him now. She had taken much from her mother: that full body of medium height. But her way of looking at one, her penetrating gaze, came from her father. So this was Philippa whose father was the cause of Nahid's death – or thus had the doubt circled around in his head fifteen years ago till he had almost gone mad during those first years he had spent thinking up ways in which to punish Michael and so avenge himself.

Mamdouh well remembered the year before Michael went away and Nahid's death, how he had abandoned himself to the idea of letting things proceed without any interference from him – 'for we are not more backward than they'. It was thus that he used to talk to himself. Yet, throughout those first years after her death, he had wished he could have had those days over again so as to change them. If that could happen he would not allow that accursed man with his ugly wife to visit them every evening to discuss literature, philosophy and culture with them – or, to be more exact, with Nahid, the Faculty of Arts graduate.

'It's all one and the same,' he said to himself in his heart, his face gloomy with grief, for Nahid had been dead and buried these fifteen years and this girl neither knew nor remembered her. 'Those days are now over and Nahid's death a matter of destiny.'

Nahid had never been unfaithful to him –

or so he wanted to believe. After her death he went on mourning her, grieving for the days he had spent with her and blaming himself: 'You killed her with your suspicions and those endless rows, accusing her of being unfaithful and torturing her in subtle ways.'

When on her bed of sickness, which she did not leave for several months after Michael had gone, Nahid would ask him: 'Why did you let him become such a friend of yours when you were so jealous of him?'

And now, after all these years, the past in its entirety had returned to him in the shape of this girl, Philippa Magoo, the daughter of his previous boss who had perhaps been the lover of his wife whom he adored and whom he may have killed.

Mamdouh came back from his long journey into the far past to Philippa's voice breaking a long silence. She was looking at him, contemplating him as though familiarizing herself with landmarks that had slipped from her memory long ago. 'My parents talked to me a lot about you. I put off my visit to Cairo until I'd finished visiting the temples of Upper Egypt. From the first instant I felt I was returning to my roots, because – as you know – I was born here.'

'The temples are marvellous,' Mamdouh said with his previous brevity. The past disturbed him and he felt uneasy about her making an appearance in his life after he had finally succeeded in coming to terms with it.

'I shall stay ten days in Cairo,' Philippa

The Visit

informed him, and from her tone he understood that she meant to stay in his flat.

Mamdouh wished it were possible for him to spare himself this visit. Reluctantly he agreed, then laid down his conditions.

'I work nights and sleep some of the daytime. You can stay here but I shall not be able to accompany you anywhere because I'm too busy these days. You can use the room with the balcony. Put your things in it and I'll ask Umm Fathi when she comes to make up the couch for you. Lunch is at about two and I leave the house around five.' Mamdouh finished hurriedly what he had to say, then asked her to follow him. 'I'll show you where the bathroom and the kitchen are, and I'll go back to sleep because it's only eight and I don't usually wake before ten.'

Philippa followed him to the kitchen and the bathroom and he showed her the room with the balcony and the couch. At the door of his room, before going inside and locking it behind him, he said: 'I'll ask Umm Fathi to make you a copy of the front-door key.' He got back into bed and proceeded to review at leisure the whole of the past.

Things changed completely with the arrival of Philippa. After less than a month it was she who would wake him up instead of Umm Fathi, she who would prepare his tea for him. She would return early from her daytime outings in Cairo to be with him before he went off to work. In fact she sometimes did not go out at all. However, her relationship with Umm Fathi went from bad to worse. She would give her orders and tell her off with the few terse words of Arabic she had acquired. When she didn't know something, she would bring out her small pocket dictionary and look out a word.

'Do this . . . it's awful . . . don't do that . . . it's awful.' She would go into the kitchen and tackle her: 'Wash these vegetables again. This glass is dirty. That room isn't clean.' The second time the servant's little boy, Fathi, had paid his weekly visit to see Mamdouh, Philippa had followed him from room to room to see he didn't play about with anything and didn't raise his voice: 'Mr Mamdouh needs quiet.'

Umm Fathi was at a loss as to how to treat this sturdy young girl. Seeing how she chased after her master everywhere, she became alarmed for him. When Umm Fathi, taking the opportunity presented by 'the foreigner' going out, complained to Mamdouh about her, he reassured her: 'She's the daughter of some friends from long ago . . . Don't pay any attention to her, she's young and these foreign women are always bossy.'

Mamdouh recollected how Michael used to manage the bank. Of a morning he would pass by the employees and leave warnings of dismissal on the desks of those who were negligent in their work. But the same strict man, how amiable he was outside work! Against his will his memories would revert to Nahid: 'You loved him more than me.' He

The Visit

would go on and on scolding her, and sometimes she would weep, sometimes rage and storm, and sometimes pray to God to free her from the hell her life had become because of two men, one of whom she loved as a friend and the other as a husband. But the position grew ever more fraught.

'Yes, I loved him – yes, and more than you,' she eventually said to him. Weary of this continual torment, she would flee in aversion from him.

Philippa fell in love with Mamdouh. Day by day she became more captivated by his detached sternness and brusque speech, for he was different from all the men she had ever met. Though he reminded her in a way of her father, she was fascinated by his aloofness, and the more she tried to break through it the more crazily in love she became. But what upset her most was his affection for this person Umm Fathi, this woman who almost shared his life with him. Because of her presence, she was unable to make close contact with him: always she was like a barrier between them.

'She's put the evil eye on you, Mr Mamdouh,' Umm Fathi, an expert in the ways of the world and of women, would say to him. 'She cannot bear Fathi and resents my presence here.' So spoke the woman who had worked for him all these years and who had always found him courteous and kind. Lately she had noticed that on many occasions this 'foreigner' would walk about the house ahead of him in clothes that were a disgrace, and would sometimes even emerge from his room, her face flushed.

Mamdouh would go on repeating to her: 'Umm Fathi, these are days that will pass.' But though the days passed the foreign girl remained boss in the house, telling her off openly in front of him, accusing her of stealing from the fridge, talking to her in a language she did not understand and turning her life into an unbearable hell.

As for him, though he saw everything, he said nothing.

Umm Fathi would plead illness and be away for three days at a time, and during them Philippa would reign supreme, not leaving him alone for a minute. She would even accompany him to his place of work and wait for him in the cafeteria of the hotel till he had finished so that she could go back with him. She would stick to him like a shadow, openly declare her love and passion for him and ask him to marry her. 'I'll leave everything to live with you,' she would say, and Mamdouh would feel that his life and peace of mind were being forcibly seized from him, while his flat was turned into a battleground on which two women fought for him. Although in the last resort he had no wish to marry again, the insistence of this girl excited him: she was handing back to him, after all these years, the keys to doors that had been firmly locked.

'Then we'll travel to Australia, to anywhere,' she would tempt him, while at the same time she would plead with him: 'But

The Visit

you don't need Umm Fathi. Until we go away, or even if we live here, I'll do the work for you. I wouldn't like anyone else to look after you.'

Under her insistence he accepted to change his time of work to the mornings – 'just to see how it is for a few weeks'. Umm Fathi wept, sure she would not be seeing him ever again. She asked him to forgive her but she could no longer bear to work under her new mistress. Nevertheless she recognized the favours he had done her in the past and would always be at his disposal should he need her. Having cooked him one of his favourite dishes, she left his service. 'Let's part good friends.' She asked that she be allowed to go and he granted her wish.

Before another week had passed Philippa had bundled up her belongings and, with the pack on her back, had left Cairo in order to continue her travels.

10

The Spouse

Siddiq read the address engraved in beautiful handwriting and assured himself about the number written to the right of the iron door with its decorations and pictorial representations. The housekeeper opened the door and politely invited him in, where there stretched before him a vast hall that ended in a glass window occupying the breadth of the wall; behind it showed a garden, which he imagined to be luxuriant. The walls were covered with valuable pictures in gilt frames, and his feet, as he walked between flowers and animals to an armchair, sank into the carpet. The woman came back with an iced drink in which were different fruits. In front of him was a wooden table inlaid with ivory; on it was an open book in which he read: 'Fire is in the embers, water in the earth, the palm tree in the date-pit.'

'Four times greeting, you are welcome.' He

rose and shook the hand of the elegantly dressed woman who stood in front of him. She sat down when he did, with the length of the room separating them. Siddiq answered, saying: 'Yes, I am Siddiq al-Nu'mani. The harvest was a full one this year, and I saw the river at the source and at the mouth; I comprehended the delta and the sea, and I have come to ask for the hand of the young girl.'

For seven years Siddiq had ploughed and sown and watered and at the time of the harvest the earth was always generous: four quarters: a quarter to the owner of the soul, a quarter to the owner of sovereignty, a quarter to the owner of the land, and a quarter to him and to the field. Seven years had passed and today he gives back to each what is his, for here is the wheat, plentiful as the sands of the ocean.

The woman pointed to a pictorial representation at the entrance in which a knight, astride his horse, had slain the dragon, and the young girl was shown.

The housekeeper entered carrying her bundled and swathed in linen, and on the pure gold neck gleamed gems of small pearls and rubies. Stretched out on a cushion of purple and scarlet and plaited reeds, she had a single hand coming from the left shoulder, and the two feet joined. There came the voice: 'The quarter, the quarter, and the broken bread.'

Siddiq knelt down, overcome by the trembling of the awaited having occurred after lengthy expectation. On the eye he saw the line of *kohl*, and the painting of lips on lips was full and rounded.

The voice reflected repeatedly off the surfaces of the polished stones, and on the breast flowed tresses of pure gold. The housekeeper returned and placed an altar alongside the open book for the burning of incense: the wood of the *sant* tree and the fragrance of frankincense. The sun was at the midway point of the rectangle of glass. Beams of light fell on Siddiq's eye and were reflected among the particles of smoke from the oblation, forming into winged names, verses, hymns.

'Seven years I sowed and reaped, and also I came to know that there is someone letting forth water from the springs in the valleys, someone who gives water to the animals of the uncultivated land, and that above there are birds of the sky, and below the insects are hearing the sound of the singing of the roots of trees. The moon has its appointed time and the sun knows to where it will return. On the twig grows the fruit, each with its own colour, and the right branch does not block the passage of the breeze to the left one,' said Siddiq.

'The explanation is difficult and the letters are sensed and imagined, and there is no affinity between the world of angels and the world of domination, nor between the world of the concealed and the world of the witnessed.' The voice burst forth from the body, the trumpet, and the book.

Siddiq kissed his bride on lips drawn on lips, saluted the aunt and the housekeeper, and left, for the agreement had been effected.

11

The Sweetness of Love

Sakina collected some firewood. Lighting it, she placed above it the pot with its contents of water and grain: 'Here is a fire with gems of blue . . . This will not be a night of rain and thereafter I shall have a full day in which I shall not know death.' Then she ascended to the bathroom on the top floor, went to the hot tap alongside the cold and turned on each of them for a particular and appropriate quantity, and the water flowed warmly. She plugged the waste opening at the bottom of the milk-white marble basin and the level of the water slowly began to rise. She looked at her face in the mirror: 'Here I am, that woman who . . .' She poured out some of the oils and perfumes, among them narcissus and jasmine, adding some of the orange-blossom water, and the water took on the colour of the sky when it is clear. She looked at her face reflected in the surface, even and unbroken like blue crystal. 'Here is Sakina whom I have known so well.' She closed her eyes as she felt her nose touching the water; then, gently, she went in.

The winter was mild and not one of the sheep had gone astray. 'Did you not see what the man living at the foot of the mountain has done to his wife? He tied her up, bare of breast and buttock, with braided flax cord to a smooth rock. He went to above the eastern hill that overlooks the river cutting through the distant valley. He slaughtered a wild goat, drinking some of its hot blood, and, with the rest, traced three parallel lines of equal length. He broke the left thigh bone, sucked out its marrow, then buried the smallest part below the lines he had drawn. He went down to the foot of the mountain where his tent was, released his sheep and sent twelve of his sons and daughters to relate the news throughout the land. He married the thirteenth child, his son, to the fourteenth child, his daughter, gave them his blessing and apprised them of the secret. He had intercourse with his wife for the last time, taking care that she should not become pregnant. He took out the bedding, household utensils, precious stones and stored food as a gift for passers-by and went on his way.'

Sakina removed her head from the water, gently dried her face and anointed it with a special blend of oil and powder so that it gave her a lively yellow colour. 'Five minutes for it to dry, five for it to stay on the skin to close the open pores, and five more for the wrinkles to be drawn out.' Sakina drew a line on each cheek, blue on the right one, red on the left. The blood coursed from the heart to the head, then again to the heart. She took a deep breath, held it for several moments, mumbled one of the attributes of Kamil, the perfect one, then exhaled it. The blood coursed from the heart to the head, then again to the heart. 'This is your man, Sakina . . . he is permitted to you. This is how he looks, this his voice, this his body.' Sakina took what her father had given her. She kissed his hand. 'This is his soul.' Sakina took what her mother had given her, kissed her hand and went on her way with her man.

She opened the plug of the basin and the water, gushing and gyrating, flowed out. She gathered up the small hairs that clung to the sides, rolled them into a ball between her fingers, then threw the ball into the wastepaper basket. 'This hair of yours is falling out, Sakina.' She gingerly pulled the yellow mask from her face so that it would not hurt her.

Kamil was muscular, of pleasing appearance, amusing, of a gentle nature. He had a soft heart and a proud spirit; he felt compassion for the orphan and pity for the needy; he was also versed in the affairs of life and conversant with its secrets. 'If this star rises amidst the constellation of the seven stars one hour of night after dusk, then tomorrow, four hours of daytime after the coming out of the sun, will be rainy. And that bird with the green stripe on the tip of its wing, if it hovers above the well three times, then before the expiry of spring we'll have a son, and he shall be like his name "Joy". Sakina, break this dry fruit and mix what's in it with three grains from this mound and anoint the child's back to stop her cough. Look at the dark colour of that cloud: a friend will visit us. This warm breeze means the ewe will give birth. Three sons, Sakina, and three daughters, and the sheep won't go astray in winter, and there will be plenty in full . . . sevens sons, Sakina, and seven daughters, Sakina, and the well won't dry up in summer, and there will be plenty in full.'

'Swift are the days of life. It is like yesterday the day my mother gave me birth, and like yesterday the day she weaned me, and the day I played and grew up, and the day I was taken as a bride to Kamil, and the day I brought forth seven sons and seven daughters.' Sakina poured some rose-water into the palms of her hands, then wiped her face. She put out the bathroom light and made her way to the lower floor. She returned to the small kitchen adjoining the rear garden, where she still retained the log fire and stored the grain and pulses. She poured the liquid that was in the pot into a tumbler of unfired clay, then sat down to sip it at leisure.

12

The Substitute

For several years I was employed in a small workshop making jewellery that was owned by a Greek named Mr Mikhali. Six days a week we would sit with a small table separating us, sawing, soldering and filing away diligently, with nothing interrupting our silence apart from the owner's amusing anecdotes about Alexandria, his relatives who happened to be still living there, and a great deal about his young wife who had died a long time ago.

At that time I was living with my mother in a small flat in Shobra. Once having returned to it after work, I seldom left it, other than to visit relatives.

During one of Cairo's hot summers I travelled to Alexandria at the invitation of Mr Mikhali to spend a few days at his flat in Ibrahimiyya. 'The heat in your flat must be unbearable,' he said to me as he gave me the key of his flat. 'It will do your health good to see the sea, Mansour.' Delighted, I thanked him. 'Don't forget to make sure the door's properly locked and that the flat's in good order.' He bade me goodbye and wished me an enjoyable trip.

This was the first time I had ever seen the sea. I was struck by its vastness and had towards it a feeling of both love and fear. Most of my time I would spend seated in front of it, watching how it would grow and then become calm, and how at night the distant lights of fishing boats would twinkle on its surface. Sometimes I would imagine myself a sailor, sometimes a fisherman, but I didn't step into it, being afraid I would drown or lose my clothes if I left them on the beach.

The flat was spacious and exceedingly clean. On my last night, after having made sure that it was in the same good order as I had found it, I packed my suitcase in readiness for an early departure. I went back to sitting on the balcony overlooking the sea as I had done on the previous evenings, watching the people walking back and forth along the Corniche and following with my gaze the beautiful girls whose hair and clothes were blown about by the breeze. At the time I was not married though I had reached the age at which virtue compels one to marry. However, both my looks and my income had not permitted me to make the venture.

Suddenly I almost died of fright as I heard someone addressing me from behind. I turned round in terror and, to my intense astonishment, found an attractive woman speaking to me in a foreign accent, which I recognized as being the same as Mr Mikhali's. To show my respect I jumped up from where I was sitting, concluding that she was doubtless one of those relatives of his still living in Alexandria. Before I was able to utter a word, she asked me about him and how he was and why he had not come with me, and whether he was intending to come shortly. Seeing my state of alarm, she asked me to sit down and be at ease and explained to me that she too had a key to the flat and that for several days she had been expecting him and had therefore come to ask about him. She informed me amiably that she did not want to disturb me and that, having rested from the long journey she had made, she would be on her way. I began to apologize for my presence, it occurring to me that she might be in need of the flat to spend the night there. I therefore told her that I had just packed my things and that I would be leaving the flat at once. She laughed at my confusion and assured me she was in no need of the flat, she herself being from Alexandria. She behaved in a friendly manner towards me, asked me for my name and mentioned various good qualities she saw in my face, which reminded her of Mr Mikhali. When I saw her taking a seat on the balcony, I stood awkwardly by the door, not knowing what to do. She invited me to sit down with her: 'The night's still young, but I won't keep you. You no doubt have an appointment.' At this I smiled without opening my mouth lest she see my misshapen teeth and be stricken with fright or distress. I mentioned to her that I had cleaned and tidied up the flat so as to leave it as I had found it. 'And I've got my things together so as to be ready to travel first thing tomorrow.'

As she had insisted I sit down with her, I did so, though I made a point of not looking at her, for she was a woman of considerable beauty. She began talking of Alexandria and the sea and of the friends and dear ones who had voyaged to various faraway places.

When some time had passed and she was certain that I was committed to no appointment, she got up and went to one of the closed cupboards and brought out a bottle with two glasses. She asked me to have a drink with her, but I excused myself by saying I did not drink. She did not insist and poured herself a glass.

The following day was a Sunday and I paid a visit to one of my maternal aunts in the company of my mother, who proceeded to tell her sister about the sea and the beaches as though it had been she who had made the journey.

On Monday morning I went as usual to the workshop. Having returned the key to Mr Mikhali, and after we had seated ourselves in our customary places, I began to relate to him everything that had occurred right up to the final night. No sooner had I mentioned his young relative who had come to enquire about him than he turned pale and insisted I repeat in detail what I had said.

Fearful and unhappy lest I had done something wrong, I told him everything. After some hesitation I informed him about her having had a drink and my not having joined her.

A number of times he asked me what she looked like and I answered him. He also asked about her way of talking and again I answered him. He enquired too about what sort of drink it had been and I told him I didn't know. He began to express doubts about what had occurred, although the details I had given him, also his knowledge of my truthfulness, gave him no opportunity for disbelieving me.

He quickly locked up the place and, taking out his wallet, gave me a large sum of money and entreated me to return immediately to Alexandria so as to make sure everything was all right with the flat, for he had had a frightening dream in which he had seen his wife urging him to join her. He himself accompanied me to the station. Before seeing me on to the train, he made a point that I should spend the night in the flat. 'Come back tomorrow, Mansour, and if my relative turns up, convey to her my regrets for not having gone there, and tell her I've sent you specially to apologize.'

In Alexandria I found the flat unchanged.

Having bought some food, I returned to it. In the evening I sat on the balcony, my gaze following the people some of whose faces I had come to know. As Mr Mikhali had expected, his relative again put in an appearance. This time, having already met her, I was not alarmed.

She came towards me as I sat on the balcony. She had changed the dress in which I had seen her last time for one that was even more elegant and attractive. As she approached, I was greeted by the aroma of a delightful perfume. She sat down in front of me, a table like the one in the workshop separating us.

Once again she began to regale me with interesting conversation about a number of matters the like of which I had never previously heard. As had happened on the previous occasion, she rose and brought out the same bottle, pouring out two glasses, one for herself and one for me.

Though I excused myself, she swore that I should at least drink a single glass, so out of politeness I accepted.

'Mr Mikhali,' she said, looking towards me, 'has really taken you over, Mansour.'

I began drinking slowly from the glass, savouring its excellent taste. When I had finished it she poured me a second glass, while she recounted to me her story to the effect that some time ago her husband had travelled to some distant place and had not till now sent for her. 'All I can do is see him in my dreams or through those he knows.'

I was greatly pained by much that she told me at that time, for this woman, the like of whose beauty I had never seen, still had such love for her husband.

Shyly I lifted my eyes to her, but she did not return my gaze. She was whispering words in a language I did not understand and calling me by my master's name.

13

The Inheritance

Murad Wassef Sawiris continued on in his car towards the mansion amidst the yelling of the children and the women's screams. And so the plan is being carried out in all its details, just as he had conceived it.

You arrive first at the town and meet the blind Suleiman, the precentor of the Church of Saint Dumyana, who still prays for you as for your father before you. You go with him to meet Dr Salim Takla, the director of the state hospital in Beni Mazar. You give Suleiman three pounds and ask him to give two to Father Matta, the priest of the church, for him to say a mass for the soul of your brother Munir. You pay ten ten-pound notes to Dr Salim for him to make out a death certificate in the name of Munir Wassef who died at the state hospital eighteen years ago. You take the papers and ask to meet Hanna Kamil, chief irrigation engineer in the province. You inform him that of course he doesn't know you, and how would he do so when he has never ever seen you. You will tell him that he is your brother from your father and that you have, after a long search, eventually reached a fact that is closer to being fantasy, which is: 'You, though you are Hanna Kamil Badie, are in fact Hanna Wassef Sawiris.'

You show him the death certificate of the brother of the two of you, Munir, from eighteen years ago and you relate to him how after the death of your father and your brother you became the sole heir. You will tell him how the late Wassef Bey Sawiris, one of the big landowners of Upper Egypt, had known another woman in addition to his wife about fifty years ago, and that this woman, may God have mercy upon her, had during that time been the wife of Mr Kamil Badie, teacher of French at the secondary school. Several years later Mr Kamil had moved to Cairo with his wife and only son Hanna. He had then died in the early sixties.

'You had then been appointed an irrigation inspector and afterwards had become a director here in the provinces. It was thus possible that the life of each one of us could proceed without our knowing the truth, except at the death of my mother, may God her mercy upon her, who informed me that my father – our father – had told her on his deathbed about this story and had asked her to keep it a secret until her appointed time on this earth should come when she would inform me.'

You are amazed at the strange circumstances of the world, you are careful about the effect of the shock on Hanna. Then you embrace him and inform him that you have decided to divide up the vast inheritance left by your father equally between the two of you.

'The law and natural justice demands it. And now, Hanna, we must settle this matter. The land, the orchards, the house, the chattels, the livestock and the mansion – everything half and half. Let's go to the Land Registry office and I shall make over to you what is yours.'

In order that the two brothers might make up for the years of being apart, Hanna moved into the mansion. Though Murad had not lived in it permanently other than for the last few years, it brought back to him many memories.

'It is here that I passed many of the summers of my youth. Then I journeyed to Cairo and lived there. I travelled abroad a lot and my father died when I was abroad but I used often to return to visit my mother. After her death I decided to move to the country estate and I lived here except for short periods when my work forced me to go to Cairo.'

The two brothers would often laugh at their memories.

'It's in the blood,' Murad would say whenever they were of one mind or they behaved in an identical fashion.

Hanna was a bachelor and was known for

his wide circle of affairs – 'That's why I didn't marry,' he would say arrogantly to Murad.

As for Murad, he was married.

'Mathilda, our cousin, is a wonderful wife, Hanna. I wish you could find a woman like her' – and Hanna would look at his brother's wife, who had retained her beauty.

'Is that plausible? There's no one like Mathilda,' Hanna would answer, joking with the two of them.

Mathilda would be in charge of the mansion but would seldom do any of the work herself.

'I don't want to become like the peasants' wives,' she would say, painting her face with make-up, 'who at thirty look as if they're in their eighties.'

She also hadn't had any children. 'Children shorten one's life.' She would take two baths a day and massage herself with butter. If she got angry with one of the workmen, she wouldn't hesitate about striking him with the first thing that came to hand. 'Animals' was what she used to call them.

'But the countryside has its delights,' she would go on to say, blowing out the smoke from her French cigarette from a mouth deeply layered in lipstick, 'for I have also got bored with big cities, both here and abroad, even London and Paris.' She would sit alongside the window, sometimes for hours on end, doing her nails or listening to soft music.

'Your wife is a fine lady,' Hanna would say

to his brother after several months of their living together, 'yet she is very bad-tempered. Today, without any warning, she almost threw a glass at me because I intervened in order to rescue a maid from her clutches.'

While Mathilda said to her husband in a fury: 'That type who's suddenly made his appearance among us, warn him of my temper and let him keep his hands off the maids.'

Murad tried to calm her down and to ask of her that they shouldn't forget that they were also cousins.

A year passed. To Hanna it seemed an age because of this woman Mathilda. How did his brother, this good, pleasant man, put up with her? This was something he could never understand. 'If I were in his place I'd have murdered her ages ago,' he used to say to his friends at the club. 'She's without doubt a mad woman.'

What made Hanna even angrier was that this wicked woman would sometimes treat Murad as though he were one of the unfortunate workmen whose miserable lot it was to be under her orders. 'This sort of woman can't be treated decently,' he said to his brother angrily one day when she attacked Murad without any apparent reason. 'Put her in a lunatic asylum, Murad, or pay her back in kind. This sort of woman can't be tamed. Either keep away from her or do away with her.'

But Murad did not pay her back in kind and would apologize to his brother.

Murad continued on in his car towards the mansion amidst the yelling of the children and the women's screams. Murad had cut short his trip to Cairo and had returned at once on hearing the news of Mathilda's suicide.

Hanna was utterly exhausted when Murad entered: he was unshaven and his hair showed white where he had neglected to dye it.

'My condolences,' said Murad to Hanna. 'I am sure the impact of the incident was very distressing. I have returned directly from meeting Dr Salim and he will do the necessary for making out a certificate of death by natural causes. Father Matta, in deference to our family, will have prayers said in the church for the soul of the deceased. I have paid all the expenses and the funeral will leave tomorrow morning at around eight. Gain control of your nerves and be strong, Hanna. You have undertaken all the difficult matters, so now go and shave, dye your hair and prepare for the morrow.'

Hanna didn't sleep the whole night. 'Why?' he asked himself again and again. After the ceremony held on the fortieth day after death he went with Murad to the Land Registry office and assigned to him all that he had inherited.

14

The *Maria*

'Let it be a necessary holiday,' I said to myself as I made my way by car towards the eastern desert instead of to the office. The temperature outside was extremely high and I was fed up with Cairo and my innumerable activities there.

I didn't have in mind any particular place: perhaps a quick visit to the Red Sea coast, or even a stay of several days. I put on some light music and made a pact with myself to switch my mind off work with its increasing burdens: reading through contracts and signing them, examining tender documents and the problems of management and employees.

So here I was reaping the fruits of the success of my company and its rapid growth. Whenever I look in the mirror that face reveals itself to me, with the increasing lines and with a tarnishing yellowness; a yellowness I had not feared until after I left the hospital several days ago.

In Suez I stopped at the telephone exchange and called my office.

'I'm on a necessary holiday.' I didn't talk much with my secretary despite her desperate attempt to understand or to disapprove. Where? Why? 'The important thing, sir, is that the tender offers are being opened tomorrow.'

'Soon, Mimi,' was all I promised her.

It is difficult for them to believe I'm in need of some rest.

I kept on southwards. The road came extremely close to the sea shore, There were many variations of blue. The sea returned to my memory.

'If you don't go out to it, it won't come to you.'

I came to a stop. I took out the thermos flask of coffee that the cook used to prepare for me every morning and sat down on the sands. The winds were hot, despite the nearness of the water. I breathed in the air, enjoying the sting of dampness. How many times had I come to this same shore and camped out with my friends! The days of youth cannot be replaced. As for now, the years were passing and one's sole occupation was that octopus called success.

I rose to my feet lest I return to thinking about work, brought on by the recollection of success.

Getting into my car I continued on my way.

A little after Zaafarana I saw a signpost to the Anbaboula Monastery. Underneath it sat

The Maria

two young men. I slowed down and they asked me if I was intending to visit the monastery.

I remembered the last time I had visited the monastery, with Françoise, my girlfriend at the time. This was just after graduating from the College of Engineering. We had spent two nights in the valley within the mountains. From it we could see the narrow alleys amongst the domed buildings of the monastery, the women in their black clothes who were allowed to enter the church, and the monks.

I asked them if they needed any water as I was on my way south. I opened the fridge and took out two bottles of mineral water. They thanked me and sheepishly admitted to me that, in this heat, they had finished the water they had with them in their water flask.

I too had walked in the desert waiting for lifts. I almost returned to tell them my story, to warn them of the frightening things that could happen, to recount to them how, only days ago, I had almost died.

'You're in need of rest,' my friend Dr Azzam had pronounced. 'This is a warning from the blood pump in your body. Your heart's saying to you: "Take it a bit easy." '

I continued driving: maybe their fate would not be similar. Before four o'clock I had entered the town of Ghardaka. How changed it was! All these new streets and buildings under construction. I saw the boards carrying the names of friends of mine, my competitors. Each had carved out for himself a piece of the future: a huge touristic project, flats and chalets, markets, barbed wire round vast areas, concrete columns, workers and cement-mixers.

At the Sheraton, once they heard my name, the person at the desk, after apologizing for there being no rooms, put me in a wing reserved for the management. 'Follow me, sir,' said one of the staff, taking my small bag.

I threw myself down on the bed. From it I was able to see some of the islands, small motor boats and sailing craft. At a distance my attention was drawn to a yacht some forty metres in length. All on its own, it was difficult to ignore. The colours of the mountains and the water were reflected on it.

'So what?' I told myself. Several years ago I too had toyed with the idea of buying a boat or a small yacht. But this yacht of forty metres! I smiled. I would have to increase the capacity of my blood pump several times if I were to be able to possess its like. Maybe, even if I were to increase its capacity, I wouldn't be able to do that.

It seems that I must have dozed off for a while, for I woke to the sound of the telephone ringing. In alarm and with an automatic gesture, I lifted the receiver. Who here would be asking for me? I wondered.

'His Excellency Sami Labib?'
'Who is it?'
'Aziz.'
'Aziz?'

The Maria

'Aziz Farah. Good to know you're here.'

Aziz Farah. The names comes to me like a wraith. Scores of years have passed since I last saw him. The last I heard of him he was living in Canada, having been outstandingly successful as a businessman.

'Hallo, Aziz. Are you in the hotel?'

'More or less. I'm on the *Maria*, my little yacht. I learnt of your having come to Ghardaka: You're invited tonight. You're very welcome.'

So this was the *Maria* about which I'd read in the architectural magazines, and this was Aziz. What times we were in! But how had he known I was staying at this hotel, when I'd been here only a matter of hours?

I almost turned down the invitation, for I was in need of rest and quiet. To accept would mean talking business, or at least boasting of the extent of one's success, for Aziz had graduated with me at the same time and was now perhaps among those who had achieved a high score in the wealth-accumulating stakes. News of him was to be found in both the local and the international press.

'Aziz, maybe it would be best to put off the invitation till tomorrow. I'm exceedingly tired.'

'Sami, I'll send you the boat at nine. How happy I am to hear your voice!'

So be it – I knew Aziz and how insistent he could be.

'It's settled then.'

Some minutes before nine there was a knock at the door.

'The boat's waiting for you, Excellency.' A young man in white trousers and braided jacket accompanied me.

On the yacht there were a number of bronzed men and women. It was in his spacious office that I met him. The years had not changed him, though he had put on some weight. He embraced me.

'Sami – just as ever.'

'And you too.'

'I've invited a few friends to meet you. It's good to see you. How I wanted to pay you a visit, but Cairo . . . I never ever go there. This here is my place of residence in Egypt. After all these years we meet at sea.'

He gave that disturbing laugh of his: it was difficult to know where it issued from or the extent of its sincerity.

'We'll have a long chat later on, for I'll not let you go tonight – I've had a special cabin made ready for you. It's a lot better than the Sheraton, but for now let's enjoy ourselves a bit. Everything's ready. I heard about the slight trouble you had. You work too hard, Sami. First you must enjoy yourself, then work. I was so distressed to hear about it . . . Do you remember the days when we were studying together? But we'll return to that later . . .'

And before I was able to ask him how he'd heard of the trouble with my health, or learnt that I was at the hotel, he had got to his feet and, holding me by the arm, had taken me up on deck, where there were now more guests.

'You must enjoy every moment of your life, Sami – you've worked quite enough. Here from the sea the whole of Egypt seems very small, even the whole world is small. I receive information anywhere I am. Do you know it's my intention to set up several touristic projects? Here in Ghardaka. Would you, incidentally, undertake their construction for me? I'm confident your contracting firm is sufficiently large. I've studied its performance and promise and believe it to be the company most suited to my needs. Or let's come to an agreement – why don't you sell it to me and sit back? I'll let you have the whole sum abroad. Enjoy it – don't leave it for someone else to inherit. Let's spend what time we have left at leisure. I take it easy now and leave the management to my assistants, now I merely make the final decisions.'

So Aziz wants to buy up my company. I used to think I'd achieved a lot, but it seems as if I've got a long way to go.

'You're mad – and be without a job?' I laughed.

'But be happy – ' and he pointed to his heart. 'It can't take any more. We'll finish our conversation later.' He smiled and filled up my glass. He pointed to a group of men and women. Among them I made out several well-known faces. My attention was particularly drawn to a woman of singular beauty; she was wearing a green dress that exposed her broad shoulders, while around her neck was a large ruby.

'Let me introduce you to my wife Nancy. This is my good friend Sami, a friend from my young days and one of the best known engineers.'

The woman greeted me very amiably and shook me by the hand.

Once again Aziz drew me towards the bar and enquired about my news with women.

'You know everything about me; you know the time of my arrival and about the crisis I went through some days ago, and you've made up your mind to buy my company. You also inevitably know the news about Nadia.'

'Don't exaggerate, Sami. It was just that I was going through the names of the main engineering companies and your name was naturally among those put forward ... Do you remember the days we used to go for trips together in the desert? How we used to visit the oases on camel? And the monasteries? Do you remember the monastery of Anbaboula and how we met up at the valley leading to it? What a coincidence it was! And at the time you had with you your French girlfriend. Do you remember her name? I still remember it – Françoise.'

'Yes, of course I remember it,' I said, hiding a smile. 'And no doubt you remember how you made up to her and seduced her, you bastard.'

Aziz laughed and showed signs of embarrassment or regret on his face.

'We were young, Sami ... they were

wonderful days. In fact, though, it was you who were the bastard. All those girlfriends! In any case, for you she was just one of many, while for me . . .'

'While for you, you were the hawk.'

'Oh no, the kite – the kite scavenging for left-overs . . . I was very sorry to hear the news that you'd left Nadia after all these years . . .'

'Let's be frank about it – it was she who left me. It seems I'm not what I used to be, Aziz.'

'And the children?'

'Basem is studying in England and Manal is in France.'

'And she?'

'She has married a businessman who lives in the States – your next-door neighbour.'

'I didn't understand why you let her have all that money.'

'The matter wasn't wholly up to me – you know women and their wiles.'

'I know . . . I know – there's always some man richer or more attractive. Let's put aside all that now and enjoy what time we have left . . . And don't forget that money allows one to make a choice. That's why I decided not to have children so I wouldn't be tied to any one woman – even to Nancy, who is more my business manager than a wife in the accepted sense.' Aziz laughed.

'She provides certain services and I reward her with a life of royalty. Today, for instance, she met these two recently married young men. She sniffed out in them the odour of the beginnings of boredom, or the desire to ascend the approach ladder to wealth, so she invited them.'

Aziz then pointed towards a radiantly pretty young girl.

'Doesn't she remind you of Nadia in her youth? If you like, be my guest. Now come along and I'll introduce you to her – or let's say, allow me to wipe out the mistake of Françoise.'

No sooner did we approach than the guests gathered round us. Many of them hastened to engage Aziz in conversation, to ingratiate themselves with him or to seek favours.

A certain feeling of dejection beset me, and I asked myself whether my decision to come to Ghardaka was a happy one. The last thing I had been thinking of was the pressure of such greetings and flatteries as I was experiencing and, in particular, entering into any battles on whatsoever level.

I was on the point of asking Aziz to have me taken back to the hotel when Nancy approached accompanied by the girl about whom Aziz had talked.

'Mr Sami, a friend of my husband's, and my friend Madame Faten. I met her only today on the beach, but it's as if we've known each other for ages.'

Nancy had a special way of talking and of looking one in the eye: a mixture of tenderness and ferocity, also without doubt a deep experience of dealing with people.'

'I've heard a lot about the projects your

company is engaged on, Mr Sami.'

Faten was no more than twenty years of age, with wide eyes and a provocative smile. She was wearing brief shorts that pinched her full thighs. She looked more at home on the yacht than most of those present. As for her husband, he had taken himself off with an attractive foreign girl and was sitting with her on a sofa far from people's gaze.

Perhaps it would be best to absent myself now, I told myself, as I felt the sweat trickling down my back. There came to me the thought that I was still ill and exhausted.

'My father's also in contracting, though in a small way.'

The ball was being thrown at me and I must return it. But this bastard Aziz wants to buy up my company. Has he gone mad, to even think of it? Does he think I'm dead? Or, with his experience, does he know I'm dead?

Cleverly Nancy noticed the state of despondency that had descended upon me. Perhaps she was dismayed by my pallor or the way I was pouring with sweat.

'Let's sit down for a while' – and she put her hand round me, as she steered me away. 'Today's exceedingly hot and you're fully dressed. This is woman's genius, she can wear anything at any time. You businessmen are poor things. You need some air-conditioning – ' and Nancy took me off to an air-conditioned cabin which had a wide bed and a table with a small bar on it and a semicircular sofa alongside a large porthole just above the level of the sea.

How did he know all these things about me? Had he become so rich he was capable of buying me up, just on a whim? Aziz Farah?

'Why don't you take off your shoes and jacket, Sami?' – and Nancy helped me to do so, for the room was going round and I was breathing heavily.

'You seem to be exhausted – it's inevitably the long journey on this hot day.'

She pushed me gently on to the sofa, put a cushion under my head and began undoing my tie and shirt buttons. I felt some relief once my chest was freed of these coverings. I took a deep breath and started to sit up while I tried to arrange my clothes. It seems that I had lost consciousness for a while.

Nancy was sitting on the carpet alongside me. I felt her fingers running through my hair moist with sweat, moving it away from my forehead.

'Don't get up, you're in your own home here – there's no need to be formal. Aziz has impressed on me that I should look after you well. It's obvious you're a good friend of his. Since I've known him I've not seen him so pleased to meet a friend as he was today when he knew you were coming.'

I wasn't dead yet. If this was a trap he'd set for me, I would not fall into it. All I dreamt of was returning to the hotel, putting out the light and sleeping till morning. And in the morning I would return by plane to Cairo.

'Thank you, Madame. Don't spoil your evening because of me. In a few minutes I'll be right as rain. Go ahead and I'll catch you up.'

'Don't get up and don't worry at all about me. It's a boring evening and it's the same every night. Aziz hasn't even noticed our disappearance. I went up on deck while you were dozing and found him wholly occupied with Faten.'

'Did I fall asleep?' I enquired in alarm, for I hadn't been aware of her having moved away from beside me.

'For a while. That's the best thing you could have done and now you seem to be a lot better.'

'For how long?'

'Maybe an hour, maybe longer.'

A whole hour and I hadn't felt a thing! This was similar to the crisis I had just been through – the same symptoms. At the office I had felt that very same sensation of weariness. I had stretched out on the couch and had woken up in the Azzam Hospital.'

'You're fine now, you seem to be in fine form.'

Nancy got to her feet and seated herself alongside me on the sofa. Skilfully, gently, she ran her fingers over my chest, stroking that little pump of which Dr Azzam had warned me.

It would have been best had I stopped over at the monastery or in the desert. How marvellous that valley was! Suddenly it seemed to me that she was Françoise. Yes, there was much that was similar about them. Years, not all that many, some years, just a few years only had passed for her to seem now . . .

'Don't be distressed, Sami. You're fine. I'm convinced you're all right. Your heartbeats have improved a lot. Your muscles are regaining their youthfulness; I feel them tensing and growing stronger between my fingers. This is marvellous . . . How handsome you are!'

'I want to meet him now.'

'What are you saying?'

'I want to meet Aziz for something important.' In vain I tried to get to my feet, but my body was not capable of it. Now I see her: she is standing with him by his car. She is laughing with him at something I don't know about. She is pouring water over his naked body, a crowning submission, and helping him to wash his back.

'Françoise.'

'Who?' she asked, removing her green dress and straddling me with her bare legs. Her breasts, freed from her bra, stroked my chest.

'I must go back.'

'How marvellous this is! How marvellous you are! Marvellous . . . Don't go back . . . You won't go back.'

In vain I tried to push her away from my chest so I could breathe. No longer did I even have the strength to breathe.

'Marvellous . . . marvellous . . . marvellous . . .'

'I . . . the company isn't . . . it won't . . .' the words issued falteringly from my mouth.

The Maria

As for her, it seemed she was no longer hearing me. She had thrown her head back and was swaying to some impact whose source I did not know.

She would appear to me, then vanish into an utter darkness.

Then she would again become visible.

Then for a few moments the darkness would increase and . . .

15

Modes of Pleasure

The Emir Najidh al-Thiqli and his torments:
 Since taking delight in pain, he found that he relished the memory of the dejection that had assailed his days and usurped his peace of mind, so that it held sway over all his feelings. Thus pain had done away with the consideration of itself, or it was as though what had occurred had not been, or as though death were a comfort after the suffering of days. Does punishment lie in the continuation of the contradiction? Has the forgiver the capacity for accepting fate? Would the point of departure be freed from what is coming from him and to him?
 So it was that the Emir Najidh al-Thiqli abandoned the throne of his kingdom, of which he was the sage, the judge and the possessor of logic and meaning, to travel with his faithful Vezir Muraji' al-Insijam to the place to which is taken he who perishes without regret, the thief and the murderer,

and he who has violated the law. He travelled to the site of suffering where he himself had previously erected the House of Reckoning and of Grief. In it is he who has abandoned his past and has repented yet does not return after the expiry of the time of change and conversion. He is punished by having rancour replaced by harmony; and he who has displayed arrogance and who has refused to recognize his nature, his life is taken from him, whether he has been there a long time or a short, without his being aware.

And she, did he not praise all her charms?

Did he not set forth the qualities of her hair? her eyebrow? and how she would direct her gaze, her nose and lips?

And did he not arrange in his imagination, when she was with him, the tones of her laughter, and her ways of speaking, and her ear and neck? Did he not say it was long? And did he not turn his attention even to her blood?

Her blood shed on his bed. Finding her with one of his slaves, he ordered his executioner to kill her. She was buried in silence and she did not return. And she was no longer named. Dejection alone remained, the dejection that suddenly assailed his days.

At first, if her spectre approached him, he would order one of his slave-girls to be brought, or he would go out hunting; and if his longing for her became too intense, he would pray and entreat, or would order a feast.

With the passing of the days, the memory of her was no longer something to disturb his peace of mind. Yet there was that terrifying thing he was no longer able to bear: his enjoyment of his pain, or rather of her pain: how her hands had clung to the bed as the head was severed from the body; the stifled shriek; the terror attending the imploring; the astonishment at the lover's cruelty.

The pain that dripped with her blood.

She, in a few minutes, after having been, was no longer.

After movement, how still she was!

She was slaughtered like a heifer. She was rubbed out by his shoe.

He sees her journeying from before him for ever.

He deems it happiness. Honour invigorates him. He almost says: 'The insect.' Yet in his pleasure he does not avert his gaze from her.

Then he pretends to have forgotten her. But what about the moment before she breathes her last? Why does he not forget that tremor that convulsed him with pleasure as she was looking towards him? Was it the look in the eyes? Or was it the utterance that the severed head did not pronounce?

A pleasure that remains with him, does not leave him.

The years pass and then, to his extreme astonishment, he finds that he has no delight in this life apart from relishing the memory of that tremor, the moment of his pain and of his victory; not the return of the pain and its assimilation, but the delighting in it, the savouring of it.

'Man dies.' How he, the sage, the physician, had consoled himself!

But he no longer knew the taste of sleep. Continued wakefulness was making him decrepit before his time. All particulars and states of being dwindled before this despotic memory, enveloping him, encompassing him, leading him from one track to another and bringing him back to where he began.

'This is not madness, rather is it your punishment,' came the cruel thoughts.

'It is merely that one of the Laws has been applied,' it is said.

'In establishing equality between yourself and those you rule lies hope of atonement for the crime. You killed as a king, and now you must be judged as a human being.'

With the reiteration of this inner thought, the Emir decided to go to his prison.

The conversation of the Emir and his Vezir Muraji' on the way to the House of Reckoning:

'Let us go back, Master.'

'But it is my destiny.'

'It tortures me that you choose me to hand you over.'

'Rather it is because of my love for you.'

'It is the House of Grief from which there is no return.'

'If the Emir has set up a House for the changing of rancour by harmony, why does he not also attempt to change his pleasure in pain for respite from the memory? Let me be, therefore, for the space of one year.'

Ja'is the Shackled:
The days and months were not easy for the Emir Najidh whom his Vezir Muraji' had handed over under the name of Qaffaf, the stealer of dirhams. Among slitters of pockets, sheep-stealers, informers, the depraved, the obscene, murderers, the hours passed gloomily. He was guarded by repressors of the unruly, his slaves for whom he had laid down their law in the methods of torture and the ways of causing distress.

How greatly he yearned for slumber, denied him by the deniers of sleep!

If hungry, they brought him water and vinegar; if thirsty, bread and bones.

And they beat him if they saw him taken by desire.

Thus the year almost passed in vain, for in the first months, being deprived of diversions and of the preoccupations of the mind, his attachment to the memory of that pleasure increased and his infatuation grew, for he was scorched by the torment of his separation from her.

The year almost passed in vain had it not been for that friendship that secretly came into being between him and one of those in disfavour. For it happened that among those imprisoned was a man in whom the Emir Najidh sought to find some gentleness and wisdom despite the suffering he had undergone and, when they were not being observed, they filched certain moments of contact.

He was Ja'is the Pryer, who never stopped investigating and questing, searching about amongst people, passionately fond of exposing human circumstances that he might learn a lesson from the grief and dejection of others.

They had come to him one day as he was exploring in one of the old libraries, his enemies having denounced him for plotting against the Emir. And to the exasperation of the repressors of the unruly, he was unbending and uncurable and would continue to look around, even among his jailers, for the conditions and causes of their happiness or grief. They cut out his tongue to stop him talking, and thus he would mumble if they appeared despondent and would heave deep sighs if he saw on their faces signs of sorrow.

They shackled him in fetters so that he would not make signs or gestures, and they shrouded his body so that he would not signal or nod.

As for Najidh, in their indifference to their captivating captive, he was able to get through to him and to complain to him about his affliction, and to whisper sometimes to him of his worries. The man would answer him with mumblings and shudderings or, if excited by what he heard, by an attempt at trilling and clucking.

In this manner did the Emir's year pass, nothing relieving him apart from his contact with his present friend and teacher Ja'is. With him alone did he begin to forget the reasons for his anger at himself, and with him his mind delighted in being happy and in forgetting his pleasure from pain, the event as well as the memory.

At the end of the period the Emir had chosen, after the Vezir had come to him on the date that he might return to the throne of his dominion and sovereignty, he ordered that the man who had been the cause of his deliverance be released.

No sooner had they unfastened the shackles from him and unravelled the shroud, than he died.

16

The Tomb

George Coolley arrived in Luxor on a Tuesday with one of the tourist groups of the Shams Company. He was transported by a carriage drawn by a horse trained to the roads leading to the Savoy Hotel that overlooked the Nile. He made sure he had a room to himself with a balcony facing the western bank. Then, because the sun appeared to be on the point of setting, and before it should totally disappear behind the mountains stretching to the edge of the Valley, George hurried to the front balcony of the hotel where many tourists had taken their places to await the descent of the sun's disc. Numbers of them were from groups of American and German tourists in the autumn of life, sipping whisky or beer and showing one another the day's acquisitions of *galabias*, cheap jewellery and imitation or fake antiques.

George ordered a bottle of Stella beer,

emphasizing the word 'Stella' to the waiter, it being one of the words he had trained himself to say by recording his voice pronouncing it. Ever since he had made up his mind to undertake the trip, he had not let slip a single opportunity from which he might derive full benefit from his visit to Egypt. He had bought books for learning Arabic, together with the records that went with them; he had read countless works on Pharaonic history and art; he had studied maps that showed the sites of the temples and gave their different names over the centuries. More important than all that, he had spent a great deal of time listening to his new friend at work, Wilbur Weidmark. Ten years older than George, Weidmark had already visited Egypt; his fascinating experiences, wide travels and distinctive personality had been among the reasons for their friendship being so speedily cemented.

Wilbur's words to him detailing his wonderful trip to Egypt corresponded to what was at present happening to George:

'You reach Luxor on a Tuesday evening after a long train journey across the Valley. It is called the Upper Egypt train. From the station you are taken by a carriage drawn by a horse that knows the roads to the hotels without being directed. These horses are driven by men burnt by the sun; they wear flowing *galabias*, have the faces of chiselled statues, and speak with an American accent.'

'What a magnificent night!' said George, talking to himself on the balcony. 'And how magnificent are the mountains stretching along the western bank!' They looked violet-coloured immediately after the sun had descended behind them. He filled another glass with the iced beer whose taste he had become fond of from the very first sip. He felt himself becoming used to the place, as though he knew it well and had an old bond with its secrets and rituals. It had even been possible for him, only a few hours after his arrival, to point to these mountains floating in that darkening light and say: 'Over there are the tombs of the eighteenth dynasty. I have become fascinated by their history and the inscriptions on their tombs and buildings.'

'On the following day – ' he remembered Wilbur recounting – 'you go to visit the Ramseum and the temple of Hatshepsut.' Both were architects and lovers of architecture.

The weather had become warm and darkness descended with unobserved slowness. The balcony was now filled with numbers of tourists and Egyptians, their voices suddenly loud with the disappearance of the noise of the sparrows that had previously filled the silence of early evening.

A party of students, drumming and singing, passed in the street. George experienced a trembling, something that came over his body whenever he was frightened or elated.

On Wednesday morning, in accordance with

the precise programme of visits in which the Ramseum and the temple of Hatshepsut were scheduled, George woke up at six, had breakfast with the rest of the group and, at a quarter to seven, was on the balcony where they met the guide who was to accompany them to the western bank.

'Ahmed al-Qousi' – a handsome young man introduced himself in proficient English with shades of the terseness of New York and the finesse of Oxford, depending on the word used or the person addressed.

Most of the group, with their loud clothing and the cameras that never left their shoulders, were American; there were also some English, who gave the impression that they had previously passed by and seen these places, also a few Japanese who had joined the group that morning because of its guide speaking English.

Amidst this large gathering George noticed a girl who had attracted his attention the previous day on the hotel balcony. Her tawny complexion had been obtained from being burnt by the sun.

On the ferry that conveyed them to the west bank he seated himself beside her. He introduced himself to her and learnt that she was from Sydney, Australia, and was on a visit to Africa; she was coming from the Sudan and was going to Greece by way of Egypt.

'I decided to stop off on a quick visit to Thebes, but I fell in love with it and I no longer know whether this is my sixth week

The Tomb

or my sixth year,' she said to him, laughing. He believed he had heard the same words from Wilbur, so he told her the story of his friend who had already done this trip.

The ferry approached the shore, which was crammed with tourists and locals on their way back to the eastern bank.

'The western bank where the Pharaohs chose to have their tombs,' said Ahmed, endeavouring to draw the attention of the members of his party so that they would not get lost among all the other groups. 'And now,' he concluded in a New York accent, which gave George the impression he was about to visit the Statue of Liberty – 'and now the members of the Shams Company group should follow their guide, Ahmed al-Qousi.'

The ferry bumped gently against the wooden jetty but, even so, many of the passengers were taken off balance. Before George's hand had reached out to assist the Australian girl, Ahmed had stretched out his hand and given her a gentle push in the back in the opposite direction to which she was falling.

'Now don't fall into the water, Betsy,' he said in the friendly tone of someone who had known her for a long time. Then he helped everyone to disembark from the ferry and cleared the way towards the car park so that the visit might begin.

On the following day Ahmed took them to

the Valley of the Kings. At the tomb of King Seti he pointed to the ceiling where the artist had represented the different signs of the Zodiac in the form of female deities, animals and symbols. The visitors took picture after picture, and the place was filled with the dazzling brightness of flash-lights. In the middle of this chaos, contained within the walls carved out of the rock and the vaults leading to more chambers, and while they were busy recording what they saw – and themselves – on sensitive film, that they might at a later date solve these mysteries and give life to the passing moment in the form of a coloured photograph, Ahmed approached George, who had begun to write some observations on a small piece of paper:

'You're American?' he asked him.

'Yes,' answered George, surprised at the question despite its simplicity.

'Without a camera?' enquired Ahmed, laughing.

'But with paper and pen,' answered George, regaining his attention.

'And you?' Ahmed asked Betsy, who had come up close to them both, thus forming a small group. 'Without even paper and pen?' He smiled then pointed to the back wall of the tomb in the middle of which was an iron door closed with a large padlock. Below it could be seen several steps disappearing into unknown darkness.

'And here – ' Ahmed directed his words at the rest of the group who, having taken sufficient pictures, had begun to gather

The Tomb

round the threesome for fear they might miss some of the exposition.

'Here is a vault whose end has as yet not been fully excavated.'

Before George's annoyance had crystallized into a feeling of hostility towards Ahmed because of his sarcastic remark, one of the Japanese asked about the possibility of another tomb being discovered at the end of this vault and about the reason for its having been left unexcavated. The rest of the group voiced their support for this question.

'Some people have tried to do so,' answered Ahmed, looking into George's eyes, 'but they failed.' Having greeted another guide who had arrived with his group at the entrance, he asked those with him to be so good as to follow him to another tomb.

On the return ferry trip the tourists collapsed on the benches, for the intense heat had exhausted them.

'They can't even take pictures – the heat's done for them,' said Ahmed in a whisper to George and Betsy between whom he was sitting. 'All they are dreaming of now is air-conditioning and whisky on the rocks.' George smiled aloofly, for this Ahmed had a derisive way with him which, though discerning, was yet filled with a certain xenophobia.

'And you, Mr George, what are you dreaming of now?' Ahmed asked him, as if reading his thoughts. George was immersed in contemplating the delicateness of Betsy's face and her long blonde hair that hung down her back and was blown about by the wind, sometimes caressing her cheek, sometimes her neck.

'I'm dreaming about the end of the vault,' George answered calmly, stroking with his gaze the body burnt from head to foot by the sun. Betsy burst into laughter, giving George the impression of someone who has not yet lost her appreciation of the genius of the white race.

'Some have tried,' said Ahmed with the same degree of calm, imitating George's Bostonian accent, 'but they failed.' He took out a packet of English cigarettes, offered them round, then lit one himself.

On the evening of the fourth day George agreed to accept Ahmed's invitation to visit his home on the western bank, together with Betsy.

On arrival, Ahmed took his leave of them and disappeared behind a wooden door in the centre of an adobe façade. From a distance it looked as though it were the wall of a temple at the foot of the mountain, the same western mountain in which were the tombs of the Kings and Queens. The sky was a pure cloudless dark blue. The sun had not set, yet the moon was radiant.

Ahmed returned and led his guests to a room to the right of the entrance. A number of low couches covered with woollen blankets had been ranged side by side. Simple and elegant, the room had a special magic. Again Ahmed left them to return with a bottle of Johnny Walker and three small glasses, which he filled to the brim. He raised his glass and proposed a toast to Luxor. Toasts followed one upon another: to Sydney and to Karnak and to the architect who had built the temple of Deir el-Bahry – toast after toast until Boston's turn came, proposed by George.

The walls were white, devoid of all decoration or painting, though on the floor was a bright straw mat. The drink and the place was as Wilbur had described.

Ahmed rose and seated himself beside Betsy for a moment, after which the two of them came towards George and sat on either side of him. Then they raised him to his feet, each gently holding him by a hand, and helped him to walk towards the door of the room. They went along a corridor, which seemed to George to be in the direction of the mountain. He passed through closed rooms and others that were open and in which members of Ahmed's family were baking bread, cooking, weaving, preparing syrups, cutting up slaughtered animals and fashioning antiques. At the end of the corridor they arrived at an iron door. When Ahmed opened it, Betsy gripped George's arm, which she had taken in hers; he felt the heat of her transfer itself to him and he was overtaken by a certain sensation of fear.

Ahmed closed the door behind them and lit his Ronson lighter so as to cast some light on the steps they had begun to descend. They reached a vast hall whose walls were decorated with paintings and engravings the colours of which had not yet dried.

George saw the most marvellous examples of what is known as the art of the eighteenth dynasty. In the corners were tables of red and black granite covered with different sorts of food. George breathed in the perfume of sandalwood and frankincense, and the aroma of the sacred lotus. Ahmed put out the lighter, for the place was illuminated by torches carried by four young girls standing in the corners. They gave out a light that was neither too soft nor too bright.

On a low bed fashioned from pure gold, George saw the most beautiful woman his eyes had alighted upon, either in reality or in dreams. She was enveloped in transparent linen that revealed the charms of her body; jewellery adorned her neck and wrists, and she diffused the odour of musk. When George looked at her, she met his gaze.

Ahmed and Betsy stayed back after they had pushed him towards her.

The woman called to him and he walked to her, stripped of all will-power, fascinated.

George felt dizzy. It seemed to him that he was hearing the sounds of Betsy having her pleasure, and he bowed down in awe.

When the woman took him by the hand to help him seat himself beside her, George felt in his hand the tiredness of someone who has tilled the fields all day, and when he embraced her he was overcome by the dizziness of an old man exerting himself.

Then George Coolley realized that he was becoming old, that he knew he was becoming old, that some years of his life were fleeing from him and that, by attaining her, these years would be taken from him to her.

With a clarity of vision George saw the woman's face becoming serene with his desire for her.

He even saw the tiny wrinkles under her eyes being dispersed the nearer he came to her.

He dreamed of something in which he was participating. He wished he had a choice. He wished it were possible for him to take that one single step backwards – something that Wilbur had been unable to do – the step that would perhaps save him and free him from his friend's words: the train journey, the hotel balcony, the ferry, the blonde woman, the western mountain, the guide, the tomb.

17

Dawania

From his first glance at me that day I presumed him to be angry – or so he gave the impression, though he used to see things in a different way.

I said to him: 'My dear friend, my master, I have till now read to you more than a thousand and one stories.' My friend's sight was so poor he was practically blind: he would see a tree as a post, a house as a cube. That way he had of looking at one, by which he would close his eyelids into a narrow slit that bisected his pupils, would demonstrate his anger. I experienced this in him if, in the telling of a story, a man was described as being evil.

I said to him: 'After all I have related to you from the words of those of former times you still doubt my good faith and truthfulness in conveying the world as they see it – and as I do.' I nevertheless used to refrain from talking about myself for fear he would judge my actions harshly because of what he heard.

He is in his seventies and I have known him since I was thirteen. My father had taken and introduced me to him thirty years ago. He was known for his uncanny ability to distinguish voices. He had lost his sight through a laboratory experiment he was doing in front of his students at the Science Faculty where he taught chemisty. It was said that it was because of his wife who was overbearing and had had a disagreement with him one day, and that he had been so confused he had inadvertently used an acid. Some of it had spurted into his face and he had been blinded.

I said to him: 'With similar considerations . . . or in the best of circumstances . . .'

He heard only fractions of a statement.

I said: 'If you don't have confidence in me or in what I say, do as you wish, but don't ask of me the impossible: And how shall I change it, how add to it, so that you approve? We are in a world that is not the world you were used to hear me speak about thirty years ago when I came to you with my father, if you recollect.'

The years passed and I became your sight, and yet you still doubt me. Me? Who am you now. (I used to regard him like my elder brother and the first heir in death's inheritance – for he, short of a miracle, will be going to the grave before me.)

How I laughed that day!

In the next-door flat there lived Habib Yahya – the most corpulent person a flat had ever encompassed. His mother had rented it for him ten or more years ago from Dawania, who was in fact none other than Inayat Daoud. In her youth she had fallen in love with drawing, but when she found it difficult to draw hands and fingers, and had shifted between the figurative, the expressionistic and the abstract, she swore she would give up colours and canvas. She then took to listening for hours to the radio, moving the knob from station to station. Then the owner of the building, her mother, had died. I had seen that distinguished lady for the first time as she worshipped the statue of a man sitting cross-legged, which they told me – I was fourteen at the time – was of the Buddha. She had given instructions in her will that her body be cremated, but she was living under a delusion, for she wasn't cremated at all but was buried in the Basateen cemetery. Inayat Daoud then changed her name to Dawania. Having inherited the building, she let out one of the flats furnished to Habib and fell in love with him – the most corpulent person to be encompassed by rooms overlooking the Nile. She used to look after him and went back to drawing and would draw his fingers. Later on I saw the paintings.

'I told you the story and you yourself added for your part the glosses and details. Your eyes narrowed and I saw the whites becoming lost in the trembling of the eyelids. At the time you asked for forgiveness and for divine mercy for her and for her mother. You requested of me to read to you from al-Jahiz's book *The Lepers, the Halt, the Blind and the Squint-Eyed,* and you loved it. I recited to you from the words of Qais ibn Asim al-Manqari:

> They left the hovering birds busily engaged around him,
> Passing between the eye-socket and the wrist.

You opened before me doors of knowledge and I became your stick and you my eyes.

But doubt, that disease, is in control of the gateways of the soul's nourishment. You accuse me of making plans to desert you. I tell you things and you hear but a fraction of them and accuse me of lying. How? And why? I am not the one to make up things. It is merely in accordance with my promise to my father who gave me life that I strive for the truth, and perform services for you, who are his friend. I see him in you sometimes and I see him for you.

Some days ago I visited the two of them and they asked me to participate with them in a celebration. In it your name was mentioned, and in the absence of Habib she asked me about you and expressed her desire to draw you – and you know all these details. But you are mistrustful, and you attribute betrayal both to me and to her. You imagine she is after me, and you take me to account for things I have no desire for. Why? You asked me to talk to her on the telephone; you took the receiver from me and you heard her talking to me while you were listening. You became angry and the veins of your eyes were tightly compressed and they became as red as if cauterized in fire. You heard words that were not hers and you accused me of being in love, and you went to the kitchen and ate to excess. I see you are putting on weight, which I hope won't do you any harm, but I fear for you that as you grow older your thighs will become fat and will rub together. I remember my promise to my father that I would take care of you and that I would be your eyes. Suddenly you smiled, reminding me that the illness of prophets is blindness and paralysis. You insisted that the image is created in the head, for if the head goes there is no image. We laughed and felt elated, and I loved life. Going to the centre of the city, I went up the bridge and saw the statue of Ramses surrounded by earth-movers digging up the streets. I returned to you and you became angry and wouldn't believe, right up to the Day of Resurrection. You reminded me that woman was created from a rib, and you reminded me that sin comes from idolatry, and you reminded me that the dead are eaten by snakes on the second day.

I implore you to set me free that I may go to some hoped for destiny I know not of. I pray that you may see, or that I may grow blind, or that Dawania may stop loving Habib or asking about you, or that my father may return from amongst the dead, or that Satan may eat with his right hand, or that a wife may bow down in worship to her husband, or that the artist may be able to draw fingers.

I imagine to myself how, if a duck becomes too fat, it may well die, before which it must become blind.

And you became angry and accused me of fabricating all the stories. Shall I change the nature of things?

Then came the day when you asked me to open for you the room of your laboratory which had been closed for tens of years, and you asked me to bring you the retort and the test tube. Your hands touched the ancient bottles, those that were empty and those that were filled with crystals. You added water to them and they bubbled and came again to life. The ingredients were blended, and the gaseous vapours ascended, and you asked me about the colours. Sometimes you laughed, then frowned, until you were finished with what was moving around in your head, and I felt the spray flying up into my eyes and the images blurring in front of me, and my eyelids narrowed into a slit.

And you asked me about the world outside, and you took me by the hand into the other room that I had not entered, and you began recounting to me what had happened and what would happen.

18

Yusuf Murad Morcos

All credit for my marriage goes to my cousin Dr Anis Salama, who acquired his education abroad and obtained a doctorate in pure mathematics from Leeds University in England.

After the death of my father, who died a year before I completed my secondary education, my uncle Salama decided I should go to his house in Cairo so that I could complete my university studies, and before the end of the same year my mother married Mr Riyad Iskandar, who was an old friend of my father's and the owner of the only chemist's shop in the town of Beni Mazar. (Mr Riyad's eyebrows joined up above his nose.)

Death snatched my father away without warning. He was attacked by a sudden sharp pain in the stomach and he went on vomiting for three hours; before the end of this time blood burst out from his mouth as he tried to throw up what was in his intestines.

It was said he had been poisoned or had eaten some poisoned food. Coughing up his intestines, my father died.

My uncle's house, with the large balcony on the front, used to overlook the Kubbeh Palace gardens, and when I was a child I would take delight in jumping over the wall of the balcony into the gardens.

'Let's hope you'll break your back, you monkey,' was how my uncle used to rebuke me each time he spotted me jumping over the balcony wall. 'Why don't you follow the example of your cousin Anis, you little devil,' said my father to me the day I fell on my arm and cried with the pain, while over there in a corner of the balcony sat Anis reading as quietly as someone not of his age. He neither laughed nor was sad.

Every summer we were in the habit of visiting my uncle and spending three weeks with him in Cairo, after which we would return to Beni Mazar where my father had his clinic: Dr Murad Morcos, ear, nose and throat specialist.

I was the only child of my father and mother just as Anis my cousin, who was my senior by a year, was his parents' only child.

Ever since I was young I had not developed a liking for reading, nor was I keen on games or fond of such hobbies as drawing, painting or writing poetry. (Anis had written a whole poem before completing his third year at the primary school and had read it out on the stage before a large audience at the end-of-year party.) Jumping was what occupied my time during my childhood.

'You have inherited nothing from your father, you oaf,' said my uncle to me the day I had cried. I was short, fair-skinned, with thick eyebrows that joined up above my nose, while my father was of medium height, dark-skinned, and had thin eyebrows.

My mother cried the day my father died, and before my uncle arrived from Cairo Mr Riyad took me on one side and patted me on the back: 'You're the man of the family now. You must pull yourself together so that you can stand by your mother. Stop crying and have confidence in God's boundless mercy. From now on you will be exactly like my own son.'

Our house in Beni Mazar was made up of two storeys, the upper one for living quarters and the lower for my father's clinic – and I had jumped from every one of its windows.

Mr Riyad had had no sons before me and my mother was his first wife.

I lived in my uncle's house for seven years. After the first year I finished my secondary school studies. I did not obtain sufficient marks to allow me to join the College of Medicine and thus fulfil my father's wishes. After long discussions and deliberations between my uncle and my mother (my uncle had not agreed to my father's marriage to my mother, my uncle's wife later informed me), he wanted me to join the Teachers' College so that I might be assured of obtaining a post after graduating and because he, being an inspector at the Ministry of Education, was in a position to use his influence to have me appointed, on graduation, to Cairo. My mother wanted me to go to the English Section of the Faculty of Arts because, first of all, I had completed my preparatory education at St Mark's English Evangelical School for Boys in Assiout; and secondly, so that I would be able to travel abroad in the future.

(My mother had obtained the equivalent of the General Secondary Certificate from St Mark's English Evangelical School for Girls in Assiout, and as her complexion was fairish and she was in the habit of dyeing her hair blonde, she was often called 'the Westerner'.)

On the day we forwarded my papers to the Teachers' College my uncle said to me: 'Listen to what I have to say, Yusuf, and don't follow the words of your mother, "the Westerner".'

During the seven years at my uncle's house not much happened. I completed my studies at the Teachers' College, in the Botany and Chemistry Section. After I had graduated my uncle used his influence and I obtained the post of science master at a preparatory school in Cairo.

During my second year at the College Mr Riyad Iskandar signed up to go and work in Algeria. He sold his chemist's shop and went away with my mother. Later, a year after I had graduated, I saw her when she came to visit me. My mother loved me a lot.

Nothing much happened in those years. I

was not specially active in any sphere, except perhaps in going off to see certain films. I had got into the habit of staying for a long time on the balcony looking at the Palace trees or being immersed for hours at a time in daydreams. I had not known any girls except for some of those who had worked for my uncle's wife, and then my relationships with them had not gone beyond repairing secretly to where they slept.

I no longer jumped.

Sometimes memories of Beni Mazar would come to me: our house, my father, my mother, the streets or the river, but they would quickly disperse – it was even difficult for me to recall to mind the features of my father or my mother without looking at a picture of them.

Then Dr Anis came back from England. My uncle's wife held a celebration. The ground was strewn with sand and bunting was put up; a fatted calf was slaughtered and gifts distibuted among the needy. My uncle published his felicitations in the newspapers, and friends and relatives flocked in so that I saw many members of my family of whom I had not previously known. The peace of the house was changed into an incessant hubbub. Anis returned, tall, smooth-haired and with ruddy cheeks. He returned with fine, elegant clothes and a Mercedes car. He opened crated boxes and produced presents: This is for you, Father, and this for you, Mother, and this for you, Yusuf; and this is for you, Kamel, and this for you, Mary, and this for you, Nadia, and this for you, Maurice, and this for you, Louis, and this for you, Auntie, and this for you, Cousin. Presents for all the family and for all friends – even for acquaintances and those who had come with them. He opened more crated boxes and produced books by the latest writers and philosophers of the age; records of classical music, foreign music, dance music; and hundreds and hundreds of photos in colour and black-and-white of himself studying, dancing, eating, visiting museums, visiting places of entertainment, visiting friends, of himself sleeping and awake. I was greatly delighted at the return of my cousin: he filled my life with joy – at everything he did and everything he saw.

Dr Anis worked at teaching pure mathematics at Cairo University. He was successful and many of the girl students fell in love with him. My uncle's wife put forward a number of girls as possible wives for him but he refused them all.

'I shall not get married before Yusuf does,' he said to his mother, laughing, as she showed him the picture of a girl from an old and respectable family.

In the same year as he returned from England Dr Anis wrote a book on mathematics, a Lebanese magazine published a long short story by him, and he appeared several times on television and spoke on the radio. (The day of Dr Anis's talk on the radio, my uncle informed me that my father had talked on the radio before I was born, on his return from his studies abroad.)

Before the end of this year, Margaret came from England to visit my cousin. She had yellow hair. My cousin married her.

My uncle held a wedding celebration which lasted for three days and gave his blessing to my cousin's 'Western' wife. I moved to a small flat near to my school in Shobra. Margaret had a white complexion and was of medium height. One day she said to me, laughing: 'I like your looks, Yusuf. The way your eyebrows join up reminds me of the Coptic paintings on the Fayyoum coffins.' That day my uncle and my uncle's wife laughed a great deal.

Seven months I spent in my flat between dreaming and wakefulness before I married. At the end of the seventh month death snatched my cousin away without warning. He was attacked by a sudden sharp pain in the stomach and he went on vomiting for three hours. Blood burst out from his mouth. Coughing up his intestines, he died.

19

Zenodotus of Ephesus

Zenodotus of Ephesus came to a stop in the text where Odysseus describes his tenth day, when he and those with him set foot on the land of the lotus-eaters, that plant which causes him who tastes of it to lose his link with the past and the desire – and ability – to return to his homeland. He did not put back the Homeric papyrus in its place amidst the thousands of others he had spent his life classifying and arranging. Instead, he folded it up and put it in his girdle. He decided to make do with that amount of work, for evening had come on.

He had spent tens of years as a curator of the biggest library in the history of mankind. He had collected, purchased, classified and ordered to be copied sufficient books to fill the open galleries and rooms with everything that had been written on knowledge in whatsoever tongue. Yet his real love was to be in the company of the verses of the blind lyre-player, the poet who sang of the genealogy of the gods and of mankind; Homer who searched for the impossible within the soul and understood the extent of the insignificance of man's life.

Zenodotus went down the stairway that extended in front of the library. Towards the sea Alexandria, city of the living and immortalized lords, sloped down. To the left of the harbour he saw the lighthouse, one of the wonders of the world, the greatest achievement of construction by his dear friend Sostratus. It was as though the lighthouse reminded him of the problems jostling in his head, so he sat down for a while on one of the broad marble steps and looked at the vast granite pillars that his friend had raised up above the top of the lofty tower housing the fire, the fire whose blaze reached up to the sun itself. Again he extracted the papyrus and read it by the brilliant light: 'The lotus, he who eats of it forgets where he is and why.' Suddenly he remembered that he had been invited for that night to the house of his assistant Alexander, a major poet. It was their weekly appointment when he would meet up with a group of scholars and men of letters. As for tonight's meeting, it was not to discuss a subject of philosophy or art but to search for a solution to the catastrophe that was imminent, the catastrophe that was about to befall his lifelong friend Sostratus. Though this brilliant architect was now advanced in years – and all lives must inevitably come to an end – there was a strong

Zenodotus of Ephesus

rumour in the city that King Ptolemy Philadelphus was wanting to put an end to his friend's life before its natural term. Rumour had it that the tower of the lighthouse, the height of which was more than one hundred metres, had not stood up to the winds and that the stones of which it was constructed were being eroded. Even worse, that below the letters of lead, each of which was the height of a man and which bore the commemorative invocation crowning the lighthouse in the name of the god-king Ptolemy, even more splendidly solid lettering was to be seen in the name of Sostratus.

Why does man's mind operate without relaxation? When will it desist, even for an instant, from doing things that are distressing and upsetting? Alongside that tragedy were innumerable matters he was no longer capable of understanding or accepting.

The rite of deifying the king, which had been started by Alexander and which was followed up by Ptolemy Soter, in accordance with the religious rules in Egypt, was converted into a demand for a continuation of being worshipped after death. King Ptolemy Philadelphus ordered that temples be built in the name of his deceased parents and that sacrificial offerings be made to them. This was the first time he had heard of it occurring in the history of his Greek or Macedonian people, for the gods had their place on Mount Olympus and their number had reached a figure which did not allow of any increase. What mountain would be large enough for them if the deification of relatives and favourites was permitted?

And the king's marriage to his sister Arsinoe, and the attempt to deify her by making her a handmaiden to Aphrodite, how can the heart put up with such burdens?

And the last edict pronouncing the deification of his mistress Belistes and his sister Philota. All will become gods.

The elderly man pulled his robe about his body to protect himself from the drizzle which the sky had begun to sprinkle before opening its doors to the rains.

Alexandria, O magnificent city! We have come to you so that we may learn, and here we are obliterating your lineaments.

Zenodotus was about to get up, but the personal problem that afflicted him, caused him to seat himself again: his daughter Selene was wanting to be her own free self and to marry an Egyptian of her choice, in imitation of the women of this country.

If we have not chosen what is beneficial for us, then who is capable of helping us?

Zenodotus fingered the papyrus. And these poems of different styles and attributed to a single writer, though he doubted their authenticity, were none the less the only work which, if saved, would immortalize his people and preserve the history of his gods. This heroic poem, inherited by forefathers, how would he gather it into a book? And if he did so, was he capable of preserving it? Especially in such an extraordinary country as Egypt? And their priests, who was capable of standing up to them, of contesting with them for power? They had devised methods that were more lasting than the written or engraved word. These temples bore symbols, and there were their prayers with their captivating tunes.

Not everything that is written lasts, not even the history of a people in their entirety. These priests, with what magic had they managed to win over Ptolemy? He had granted them the right of worship, had exempted them from taxes, had given them lands, and had let them pray for him in a language he did not understand.

And the truth, was he searching for it in works of tragedy or comedy? Or did the truth lie in their ability to acclimatize? How had they divested themselves of the novelty of compilation and creation? They made do with repeating and conserving what had come down to them from thousands of years. The heads of animals and birds were still crowning their feast days. The gods in their view were far above humankind, and even though they deified their kings, that was only to win over man's weakness before the dream of eternity. And the individual of this nation that believed without questioning, the peasants who through their sweat were filling the treasure houses of the empire, and by which his very own library had been set up, the library of Alexandria, he had found to be happy. They still tilled the soil, even if they had become second-class citizens, even if forced to worship their new kings – these were but names added to or deleted from the list of deities.

Oh, the times of depression, times of uncertainty between him who believes he knows and him who in his happiness does not know.

Zenodotus rose to his feet, having resolved where to go.

But oh, the times of depression that made him lose his way among the streets of Alexandria, streets in which it was difficult for someone who hadn't been drinking to get get lost – and he had not yet drunk anything.

Where am I? he asked himself after reaching the north of the city and finding himself among the port's warehouses.

Thinking is the root cause of being in a stupor. Even the plan of the place, a plan he had ordered to be copied out hundreds of times, had slipped his mind.

Under a high wall, several workmen who were warming themselves round a fire caught his attention, or it might have been the smell of burning that he noticed. Prompted by doubt, he approached them. Right before his eyes, as he had expected, he saw thousands of papyri, rolled up and sealed, dessicated by the passage of the centuries.

The first thing that occurred to him was to put out the fire. Forgetting his worries, he wished that he might be mistaken. He hastened to stamp down the brittle embers. He took off his coat and threw it down against the wind.

The voices of the workmen, between fear

and surprise, came to him. It was more fear that guided them, for both his clothes and his appearance indicated that he belonged to those who ruled. They were of his nationality or of nationalities related to his. He ordered them to bring him a torch and he sat down and collected the charred remnants. He heard them pleading excuses for an offence they were ignorant of. Perhaps it was indolent guard duty, or the bad smell of the fire, or any other reason, for, like him, they were new to this city and hadn't yet committed to memory all its laws. They had come some time ago in order to depart if they made money, and they had stayed on.

Was it the lotus, O Zenodotus? Or was it the tenth day?

He began gathering up the scraps of papyrus written in hieroglyphics, demotic, Greek, Persian, Hebrew and different languages. By dint of knowledge acquired through experience, a heart-rending surprise came over him.

They were recently acquired, copies that had been transcribed by the hands of hundreds of scribes who worked under his command at his library, the library of Alexandria. Between his fingers he felt the seal that he had originated for assuring the faithfulness of the transcript, so that it might be preserved for history, wholly in conformity with the original, even if the original were to be lost.

He did not know how much time had gone by. It seemed that the rain had stopped. The smell of the sea came to him, and from time to time the faces of those around him and the piles of papyri were lit up by the lighthouse.

The recollection of his friend Sostratus, and of his assistant Alexander, and the appointment he was on his way to, slowly came back to him.

He rose sluggishly to his feet and ordered them to collect up the scraps of paper and deliver them to the library on the following day – however small the scraps, he confirmed to them.

He didn't ask them how they had come by them. He uttered not a word of censure. He wrapped his cloak round his body and continued going further north, towards the sea itself.

He continued feeling the cold water rising around him.

20

Love Letters

I was informed by a rich friend that an elderly woman, an acquaintance or relative, wished to receive love letters in exchange for a generous fee. As at the time I was completely broke and unable to find a publisher for any of my writings, I agreed.

I presented myself to her in his flat in accordance with the appointment that had been fixed.

'May I present Emil Mawafi, a celebrated writer.' He was silent for a while, then continued in an attempt to raise my rate of payment: 'Although he is still, by reason of the singular delicacy of his writing, relatively unknown, I must nevertheless admit to having read in his works the most beautiful things to have been written about sex.'

The woman looked at me with half an eye – or as far as her right eyelid was able to rise.

I would have liked for her not to have heard or seen me, but against my will I gave a slight smile and she extended to me the oldest of living hands. My friend nudged me and, understanding, I kissed it.

'Madame Insaf Hanim Zarie,' my friend completed the introduction.

The woman invited me to sit down. I took my place near to her, without going too close, as I tried to weigh things up: should I venture on this assignment or content myself with the meeting?

'Emil Bey.' The woman cut through the thread of my thoughts as she now looked straight at me, after having opened her left eye which had up till this moment been closed and which, it seemed to me, had a brightness whose origin I found difficult to explain. 'Ismail Bey has spoken to me of you and the great sensitivity of your feelings, something that I miss in today's writings.'

'Insaf Hanim, Emil Bey does not so much write as give life to words.'

I was delighted by Ismail's description and felt embarrassed, especially as he had read only one or two of my early stories, which were perhaps marked by a certain number of symbols and allusions that were sometimes openly shocking though for the most part they were implied without being overtly sexual. Besides, this was old history, many years having passed in between. After my continued attempts at writing, I had contented myself for a long time with historical narratives or detective stories. These too had not met with any success worth mentioning.

Before I once again sank into the sea of delving into my memories, Insaf Hanim brought me back to the purpose of the meeting.

'When would you like to allow me to enjoy your letters?' She was open and frank and left me no opportunity for hesitation.

'At the first opportunity, Insaf Hanim.'

'And here's a sum on account.' I was extremely embarrassed as I took the hundred pounds, which it seems she had had ready and had kept separate in a part of her snakeskin handbag.

'But my condition is that you let yourself go, Emil Bey. Don't curb your imagination or allow yourself to be timid – I adore outspoken writing.'

She smiled again, having closed her eyes, then ordered me:

'I shall expect a letter from you every week; this is my address.'

She handed me a piece of paper on which were written in beautiful handwriting her name and address. Before the meeting ended she asked me not to address her by name in the letters but simply to start each one with some term of endearment.

A long time passed during which I would send a weekly letter to Insaf Hanim, and, in accordance with the arrangement, she would promptly send me the agreed sum through Ismail.

At first it was difficult for me to write. It

proved no easy assignment and on a number of occasions I almost stopped sending the letters. The notion behind the writing of them, and my compunction about having accepted such an offer, also my feeling sometimes that I was either exploiting the emotions of this elderly woman or that I was complying with an unnatural request, this feeling would often upset me. But in the end I began to persuade myself that I was a writer, and that if writing was my chosen way of life, maybe this was my sole book to be read with sincerity and eagerness, and that perhaps through such work I would – later on, naturally – take my place among the famous authors. So, gradually, I found myself deriving pleasure from sending these letters, and would in fact await impatiently the passing of the days of the week until the appointed day would arrive for me to take what I had written and put it inside the envelope that I had now begun to embellish in various ways on the outside. Many a time I would let fall on it a drop from one of the varieties of sweet-smelling oils I had bought: violets, the thousand flowers, lotus, musk and amber in the winter and autumn. As for spring, it would be the scent of orange blossom and Arabian jasmine that would cling to my letters. And many a time in summer I would let fall upon them the exquisite nectar of the flowers of the mango or the banana.

And just as my imagination devised the most beautiful of appropriate perfumes, so with the passage of time my words burned with such a blaze that my whole attention was given up to my intimate communion with this lover, sometimes calling her my eyes, sometimes my lips, sometimes alluding to her as the morning dew and sometimes speaking to her in sorrowful riddles.

And so things continued until I received my first and last letter from her. In it she informed me that she was at death's door and asked me, on receipt of it, to stop sending her any more letters. She also let me know that she would be sending me, through my friend, a sum of money which would provide for me until I was able to find another means of earning a living.

I don't know why it was that at that moment I feared death and craved for knowledge. More than anything else I wanted to see her.

Late one summer's night I hurried to her house and knocked at the door. A man in control of his faculties opened the door to me, looked at me closely, then asked who I was and what I wanted. I was frightened to speak. He himself spoke and asked me if I were he. I said: 'Yes, Emil Mawafi.' He was about to close the door when I heard her voice from inside inquiring who was at the door. I shouted out that it was I. The man grudgingly permitted me to enter and led me to her room.

She was more advanced in years that any human being. Before I was able to collect my scattered wits there rushed towards me a young woman more feminine and attractive than any I had seen in my life. She had pushed open the closed door of the room when she had heard my name. She took me in her arms and began calling me by all the endearing terms with which I was familiar. She went on kissing me and clasping me to her. She was strong and I felt so much pain in my ribs and chest from her excessive sexual ardour that I feared for my life. She went on touching my face and body, and whenever I tried to release myself from her, she would mutter frantic words and begin crazily grasping at that which I had been telling her about all these years.